Honey Bunch
AND Norman

ON LIGHTHOUSE ISLAND

By

HELEN LOUISE THORNDYKE

NEW YORK
Grosset & Dunlap
PUBLISHERS

D0101187

CONTENTS

CONTENTS

Honey Bunch AND Norman

ON LIGHTHOUSE ISLAND

CHAPTER I

LUCKY

"SUCH a funny noise!" said Honey Bunch. "What can it be?"

She ran to the window of her bedroom and looked out. Nobody was in the yard.

The little girl went back to playing with her dolls. She had seated them around her play table and was having a tea party with them. Mother had bought her a beautiful set of doll dishes, made from shells.

"Goodness, Eleanor," Honey Bunch said to her favorite doll, as the noise began again. "What *do* you s'pose that can be?"

This time Honey Bunch ran into her mother's bedroom and peeked out the window to the front sidewalk. Still she saw no one. The noise stopped, and Honey Bunch went back to her tea party. She thought she had never seen such cunning plates and cups and saucers as these were.

"They're made from such teeny, tiny shells," she said to Eleanor, who was seated beside her.

1

Then she heard the noise again. Whatever could it be?

She decided to ask Mrs. Miller, the laundress, about it. But when she went downstairs, the noise was coming from the front porch!

Honey Bunch opened the door. Sitting on the steps was her playmate, Norman Clark. He was holding something to his mouth.

"Hello, Norman," said Honey Bunch. "What's making that funny noise?"

Norman tried to tell her, but the words sounded like "Bub ib a grub bibul!"

Honey Bunch laughed. "I can't understand a word you're saying."

The little boy took the object out of his mouth and said, "This is a shell whistle."

He handed the whistle to her, but said she could not blow it.

"Why not?" Honey Bunch asked. "I'll wash it off good."

"I mean you don't know how," said Norman. "You have to have a lesson on how to blow a shell whistle. It's very special."

Honey Bunch wanted to know why he could not show her right then, but Norman seemed to want to keep the matter a secret.

"Maybe I'll show you sometime," he said, making a tremendously loud sound on the shell whistle.

Honey Bunch's cat, Lady Clare, who had just come around the corner of the porch, leaped out of sight at the sound. Honey Bunch did not think it was nice of Norman to scare her cat.

"Norman, you're a two-and-two child," she said.

"What's that?" the little boy wanted to know.

"Well, I'm not exactly sure," said Honey Bunch, "but Mrs. Miller says that's what you are."

Now Norman liked having secrets himself, such as how to blow a shell whistle, but he did not like Honey Bunch to know something he didn't. He was a little worried about being a two-and-two child.

"When did Mrs. Miller say I was that?"

Honey Bunch tried to remember all the times Mrs. Miller had mentioned being annoyed with Norman. He often came into the Morton kitchen and took freshly baked cookies, and he liked to tease Lady Clare. Not long before, Honey Bunch's daddy had bought her a police puppy. She had named him Mr. Reilly, after the nice policeman on the corner. Norman had already begun to tease the puppy.

"Mrs. Miller says you're a two-and-two child when you make a lot of noise," the little girl explained.

Honey Bunch was just about to ask Norman again to show her how to blow the shell whistle, when a car stopped in front of the house. A boy in a uniform walked toward the two children.

"Is this the Morton house?" he asked.

"Yes," Honey Bunch replied. "Have you a telegram for my daddy?"

The boy said he had a telegram, but it was not for the little girl's father. He took it from his pocket and read:

"Miss Honey Bunch Morton."

"It's for me!" cried Honey Bunch, jumping up and down.

The boy looked down at the little girl. Seeing that she was only about six years old, he asked

4

her if she wanted him to read the telegram to her. But Honey Bunch was sure the message inside must be very private and very important.

"I'll ask Mrs. Miller to read it to me," she said, thanking the boy.

She ran into the house, Norman following. He was so excited about Honey Bunch's telegram that he forgot all about his shell whistle. He also forgot to ask Mrs. Miller what she meant by his being a two-and-two child.

"Mrs. Miller! Mrs. Miller!" Honey Bunch called out as she ran toward the kitchen. "Please read my telegram to me."

Mrs. Miller was making apple cake for dinner. She put down the spoon at once, looked at the telegram and said:

"This is from your friend Flyer Frank."

"Oh, goody!" cried Honey Bunch. "What does he say?"

Flyer Frank was a young man who at one time had worked in Daddy Morton's office. Then he had become a flyer, so after that Honey Bunch always called him Flyer Frank. She liked him very much.

"Is he coming to see us, Mrs. Miller?" she asked excitedly.

"It doesn't say exactly that," Mrs. Miller replied. "Flyer Frank wants you to meet him at the Barham airport. He wants you to see a famous dog."

"Is it his own dog?" Norman spoke up.

"No, it's a dog named Lucky," Mrs. Miller replied.

Lucky, she said, was a wonderful collie dog. He belonged to a doctor who flew to faraway places to take care of sick people.

"He won't take any patients in town," Mrs. Miller explained. "He likes to help people who live in places where they don't have any doctors."

Honey Bunch thought that this was wonderful.

"Is Flyer Frank going to take me in his plane to see the doctor and his dog?" she asked Mrs. Miller.

"No, Dr. Hopewell and Lucky are landing in Barham at three o'clock this afternoon, and Flyer Frank will be there about the same time."

"Oh!" cried Honey Bunch. "Please, may I have my lunch right away!"

Mrs. Miller was puzzled. Honey Bunch had eaten her breakfast only a little while before.

"Surely you're not hungry," she said.

"No, I'm not," Honey Bunch answered. "But

6

after lunch it's afternoon and if I eat now, it'll make afternoon come faster."

Mrs. Miller laughed. "That's the way a little girl might figure it, Honey Bunch," she said, "but Flyer Frank won't reach Barham until three o'clock, no matter what time you eat."

All this time Norman Clark had stood by silently. The little boy had felt very set up about having a new shell whistle. But now his playmate was going to do something much better than blowing on a shell! Norman began to feel very sorry for himself.

"Where's Mr. Reilly?" he asked suddenly.

In the morning's excitement Honey Bunch had forgotten all about her own police pup. He had gone out after breakfast and she had not seen him since.

"We'd better find him," said the little girl.

Norman went outside and began calling Mr. Reilly at the top of his voice. Suddenly Mrs. Miller remembered that she had let the pup into the house only a few moments before.

"I forgot all about him," she said, and called out the kitchen door, "Norman, Mr. Reilly's in here; stop your yelling!"

But this time Norman's yelling did some good. Mr. Reilly, who had been upstairs, came racing down the front stairway and out to the kitchen.

"Oh, you naughty dog!" Honey Bunch cried. "What have you done to Eleanor?"

The police puppy stood before his young mistress, wagging his tail as fast as he could, and holding the doll in his mouth.

The little girl tried to take the doll away from him, but he held on tight. Then Mrs. Miller took a hand and rescued Eleanor.

Norman laughed when he came in and saw how Mr. Reilly had shaken up the doll. Honey Bunch was not surprised. Norman lived in the house back of the Morton home and the two children had played together since they were babies. Because he was not going to see the famous dog, Lucky, Honey Bunch said:

"Would you like to keep Mr. Reilly and play with him while I'm at the airport?"

"Gosh, that's swell," said Norman, his eyes sparkling. "Come on, Reilly." Norman did not like to use the word "mister" in front of the dog's name.

The little boy got the puppy's leash, snapped it to Mr. Reilly's collar and went outside with him.

Honey Bunch would have gone, too, but she decided to stay and watch Mrs. Miller fix Eleanor. Furthermore, she wanted to spoon out the apple cake bowl after Mrs. Miller put the cake into the oven.

Suddenly Honey Bunch had a thought. "Who's going to take me to the airport?" she asked. "If Daddy and Mother don't come home, I can't go," she added fearfully.

Mrs. Miller smiled down at the little girl. "Now don't you worry," she said. "If they don't come home in time, I'll take you out there myself in a taxi."

Honey Bunch hugged her. "You're the nicest person," she said. "You're salt and pepper!"

The laundress laughed. She knew what Honey Bunch meant. She had once told the little girl that she had the nicest grandmother in the world, and had used an old saying about her that she was "the salt of the earth."

9

Honey Bunch could hardly wait for three o'clock to come. Her mother arrived home by lunchtime and was told the big news of Lucky's arrival.

"That is news," Mrs. Morton agreed, "and I hope Flyer Frank will not have to leave immediately."

"He's going to visit us, isn't he?" Honey Bunch asked.

"We'll certainly ask him."

Mrs. Morton told her small daughter that the dog Lucky had rescued several people, both on land and from the water.

"There are stories about him in the newspaper every once in a while," she said. "Only last week he saved a little girl from drowning. She had wandered away from her house and started to play in the water."

"And her mother wasn't there?" Honey Bunch asked.

"Nobody was around," said Mrs. Morton. "Of course, nobody should ever go into the water all by himself, no matter how good a swimmer he is. So many things can happen."

"What happened to the little girl?" Honey Bunch asked.

Mrs. Morton said that fortunately for her,

Lucky had come running along the beach and seen her struggling in the water. So he had jumped in and pulled her to shore. More than ever Honey Bunch wanted to see the wonderful dog.

"He must be scrumptious," she said. "And Mother, may we take Norman with us this afternoon?" the little girl requested.

"If Norman will promise to be very good, we'll take him," Mrs. Morton agreed.

Honey Bunch hurried off to tell her playmate the good news. Norman still had Mr. Reilly on the leash and was playing with him. When the little boy heard he was to go too, he went round and round in a circle. The leash went round and round too, and in a moment he and Mr. Reilly fell *kerplunk* to the ground.

Honey Bunch laughed. "Mother says you'll have to be extra-special good," she told Norman.

Norman said he would be as quiet as when he had had the mumps. At half past two he appeared, clean and dressed up, ready to go. He asked if Mr. Reilly might go along, and Mrs. Morton thought that this would be all right. The pup would be left in the car while they went to meet Flyer Frank.

As they neared the airport a plane was circling overhead.

"I wonder if that's Flyer Frank's plane," Honey Bunch said.

"I think perhaps it is. We must hurry," Mrs. Morton replied.

She parked the car and started off with the two children. Suddenly Norman remembered he had left a package on the rear seat.

"It's a special present for Mr. Flyer Frank," he said.

The little boy dashed back to the car and got it. Then they hurried to the big building to watch the pilot come down.

As they stood waiting, Honey Bunch suddenly shrieked. The plane was on the ground now, and taxiing up to the building. Running out, right in the path of it, was a small dog. Honey Bunch put her hands over her eyes and cried out:

"It's Mr. Reilly!"

CHAPTER II

ISLAND CHILDREN

HONEY BUNCH buried her head against her mother's arm and began to sob. Norman Clark began to cry, too. He had let the police puppy out of the Morton car, never dreaming that Mr. Reilly would get in the way of the airplane.

Suddenly Mrs. Morton said, "Oh, my goodness! Look!"

Honey Bunch was afraid to look. Something dreadful was going to happen to her beloved little dog.

"Look!" said Mrs. Morton again. "See that big dog racing over!"

Honey Bunch opened one eye. The sight she saw made her open both eyes wide, and she began to jump up and down excitedly.

Racing onto the runway was a beautiful, big collie dog. He whizzed across the strip like a tawny streak. An instant later he snatched up Mr. Reilly in his teeth and ran with him out of the path of the plane.

13

"Oh, Mother!" cried Honey Bunch. "He saved my puppy!"

"Yes, he did, dear. And it's my guess that the big dog is Lucky."

"The one I came to see?" Honey Bunch asked. She could hardly wait to thank Lucky.

Norman was very happy that Mr. Reilly had been rescued. He realized that the puppy could have been badly hurt.

Honey Bunch and Norman were always having adventures. Recently they had made a Hi Diddle Diddle float and had won first prize in the Barham May Day Parade. During the parade Mr. Reilly had been stolen and many exciting things had happened before the puppy was finally found.

But in all her adventures never had Honey Bunch been so terribly frightened as when she saw her puppy running in front of the airplane. By this time the plane had taxied to a stop. Out jumped Flyer Frank.

Honey Bunch raced forward to meet him. Instead of smiling, the handsome young man looked very serious. Honey Bunch guessed what was the matter.

"You didn't hit him, Flyer Frank," she cried out. "Lucky saved my puppy!"

"I'm glad," said Flyer Frank. "I sure had a scare."

He greeted Mrs. Morton, then turned to Norman. "Have you been a good boy?" he asked.

Norman looked up uncertainly. "I let Mr. Reilly out of the car. Honey Bunch says I'm a two-and-two child," he said sadly, "and I guess I am."

Flyer Frank and Mrs. Morton wanted to ask Honey Bunch what she meant, but first they thought it best to go over and get Mr. Reilly.

The big brown-and-white collie had set Mr. Reilly on the ground, but was standing guard over him until someone came. Honey Bunch ran to her puppy and picked him up.

"You were naughty to cause so much trouble," she scolded, hugging him. "Thank you so much, Lucky, for saving him."

She set her puppy on the grass. Then bending over, she gave Lucky a very tight squeeze. The big dog licked her face, then put up his paw to shake hands.

By this time a little crowd of people had gathered around. But Lucky did not wish to be fondled by anyone else. He trotted off quickly to the back of the airport building.

"I guess Dr. Hopewell must be in there," said Flyer Frank. "Come on, we'll find him."

Honey Bunch took hold of the pilot's hand and skipped along. She had to go very fast to keep up with the young man's long strides.

"Flyer Frank," the little girl said, looking up at him, "you're coming to visit us, aren't you?"

Mrs. Morton, who was hurrying along behind them with Norman and Mr. Reilly, said, "Yes, Frank, you must come and spend some time with us."

The pilot grinned and thanked both Mrs. Morton and Honey Bunch.

"I'll have dinner with you if I may," he said. "Sorry I can't stay any longer, but I have a new job. I'll tell you all about it. Honey Bunch, you will be particularly interested and Norman, too."

Both children wanted to know at once what the young man's work was. But he would not

16

tell them yet. It would have to wait until dinner-time.

This did not suit Norman at all. He liked to hear things firsthand. Since he was not having dinner at the Morton house, he would have to wait until Honey Bunch told him later. Maybe he wouldn't even find out until tomorrow!

"I guess that's what I get for being a two-and-two child," Norman thought woefully.

They reached the rear door of the building and went inside. Flyer Frank looked around. He did not see Lucky's master, Dr. Hopewell. But Honey Bunch had seen the dog's beautiful, plumy tail disappearing around a corner.

The little girl pointed out where the dog had gone. They followed him and in a moment they found a man seated on a bench. He was only a few years older than Flyer Frank, and very tanned. He had big, laughing blue eyes. Honey Bunch liked him right away.

"Well, hello, there," he said, rising to shake hands with Flyer Frank. "Good to see you again. What's this I hear about your flying to the Islands?"

Honey Bunch listened carefully. Perhaps now she was going to learn about Flyer Frank's new job!

"It's a great job," the young pilot answered, "and very exciting sometimes."

He turned to the little girl's mother. "Mrs. Morton, I'd like to present Dr. Hopewell. And this is Honey Bunch, the little girl I told you about, doctor, and Norman Clark."

After he had been introduced, Dr. Hopewell sat down again on the bench. He put one hand on Norman's shoulder and with the other pulled Honey Bunch in front of him.

"Frank thinks you're the finest little lady in the country, Honey Bunch," he said. "I understand you once helped to save his life."

"I'll be very glad to rescue you, Dr. Hopewell, if you ever have to be," the little girl said, smiling back. "But please don't get into any trouble."

"I'll certainly try not to," the doctor promised.

Flyer Frank asked him how long he was going

to be in Barham. The doctor said he was waiting for a package of rare medicine which was due to arrive on Saturday from a distant country.

"I'm going to fly it up North to a little sick girl." He turned to Honey Bunch. "She's just about your age."

"I'm sorry she's sick," said Honey Bunch. "Why does she live so far away?"

"Her father is a hunter. He gets furs so ladies like your mother can have fur coats to wear," the doctor told her.

"Is there lots of ice and snow where the little girl lives?" Norman spoke up.

Dr. Hopewell said yes, indeed, there was plenty of it most of the year. Right now, it was not hard to land with an airplane where the little girl lived, because it was summertime. There were beautiful flowers and green grass growing everywhere.

Honey Bunch was puzzled about one thing. "If you don't have an office and all your sick people are far away," she asked, "how can they tell you when they're sick?"

"By radio," Dr. Hopewell answered. "The people have someone go to the nearest radio station and send a message. I pick it up in my plane."

19

"Is your plane here?" Norman asked.

Dr. Hopewell said it was, and that while he was waiting for the medicine to arrive, he would fly to help sick people on the Islands.

Suddenly Honey Bunch remembered what the big collie had done for her. She looked straight at Dr. Hopewell and thanked him for having Lucky save Mr. Reilly's life.

"Lucky's just about the best dog in the whole world, I guess," said the little girl. "I love him."

"I'll have to agree with you there." Dr. Hopewell smiled. "And by the way, I didn't send my dog to save your pup. He did it all by himself."

The doctor told the children several stories about Lucky. Honey Bunch did not know which one she liked best, but Norman had no doubt in his mind. It was the one about the burning barn.

"Two horses were trapped inside," the doctor's story went. "Lucky leaped through a window and pushed up the latch on the door so it would swing open. Then he barked at the horses' heels until he made them run away from the fire and out of the barn."

"Oh, he's wonderful!" cried Honey Bunch. "Where did he go? I want to see him again."

Dr. Hopewell led the way to his airplane. Lucky was sitting up in the pilot's seat looking around just as if nothing had happened at all.

"Lifesaving is all in a day's work for him," his master said proudly.

Dr. Hopewell turned on the receiving set of his radio. Several things came over it which the children did not understand. But all of a sudden they heard the words:

"Calling Dr. Hopewell! Calling Flying Dr. Hopewell!"

Honey Bunch and Norman stood very still and listened. The doctor picked up what looked like a telephone and said:

"This is Dr. Hopewell."

A short conversation followed. Honey Bunch could not understand all the big words in it, but she did learn that someone was ill and wanted the doctor to come.

"I'll be there," the doctor promised, and put down the receiver.

"What about the sick little girl who needs the medicine you're waiting for?" Honey Bunch asked.

"Oh, I'll have to start North just as soon as the medicine arrives for the little girl," Dr. Hopewell said, "but this trip won't take me very far away from Barham."

Honey Bunch was glad to hear this and said

she would like to send one of her dolls for the little girl to play with when she got better. Flyer Frank could bring it back to the airport that evening.

Lucky offered his paw to say good-by. Honey Bunch gave him a hug and whispered in his ear, "Thank you, Lucky, for saving Mr. Reilly."

On the way home, Norman gave his little gift package to Flyer Frank. It was the shell whistle that had made such a strange noise!

"I'll show you how to blow it—when we're alone," said Norman importantly. "The whistle is just meant for boys."

Flyer Frank thanked him and said he believed the whistle would come in handy to call his children together. Honey Bunch looked at the young man in surprise.

"I didn't know you had any children," she said.

"They are not my own children," he said, laughing. "But I'll tell you all about them after I learn how to blow this whistle."

Norman insisted that Flyer Frank come to the Clarks' back yard for the lesson. So when they reached the Morton house, Honey Bunch and her mother went inside alone.

The little girl ran to the kitchen to tell Mrs. Miller all about what had happened at the airport. Then she asked:

"Are we going to have something extra special for dinner?"

Mrs. Miller, who never forgot what visitors to the house liked to eat, replied, "We're having roast beef with lots of gravy."

Honey Bunch was glad to hear this. She liked roast beef, too. And there were always bones for Mr. Reilly to gnaw and bury in the ground.

Just before dinner was served, Honey Bunch went to her room and picked up a pretty baby doll. She ran to Flyer Frank with it.

"Please give this to Dr. Hopewell to take to the little sick girl up North," she requested.

"I certainly will," the young pilot promised. "That's very kind of you."

During dinner the young man told the Mortons about his work.

"Those children I told you about, Honey Bunch," he said, "are school children who live on the Islands."

"Islands?" the little girl asked. "You mean those pieces of land with water all around them?"

"Yes," said Flyer Frank, "and since these islands are not in a river or a lake but right out in the ocean, nearly every island has a lighthouse on it. My children live there with their daddies and mothers."

Honey Bunch had seen pictures of lighthouses, but she did not know much about them. So she asked Flyer Frank to tell her about them.

"There's often a good deal of fog over the ocean," he explained, "and the men who steer the ships would run right into the islands if they didn't have some way of telling where they are. So high towers are built, and a very bright light is placed in the top of each tower. At night the lights are turned on. Each light has a different way of signaling, so that the captain of a ship can tell which light it is.

"For instance," Flyer Frank continued, "the

24

light on Shell Horse Island flashes long—short—short—long."

Honey Bunch wanted to know if Shell Horse Island was one of the places Flyer Frank went to. He said it was and added:

"It is one of the most dangerous places for ships on the coast. It is a very rocky place and every once in a while in a storm somebody comes to grief at Shell Horse Island."

"What do you mean?" the little girl asked.

"Sometimes waves get so high they go right over a ship. And right over the Island, too. Then the giant waves dash the boats against the rocks," the young man told her.

"Oh, how dreadful!" said Honey Bunch.

Flyer Frank talked about something else. He told Honey Bunch that a couple of years before, the Government had decided to fly the children from Shell Horse Island and the other islands to the school on the mainland. They attended school in the town of Sunrise Beach.

"That's my job now. Every day I take them back and forth," said Flyer Frank. He turned to Honey Bunch. "Maybe someday you can come to Sunrise Beach and go on one of my trips with me."

25

CHAPTER III

THE SHELL HORSE

"OH, MOTHER! Daddy! Can't we go to Sunrise Beach right away?" Honey Bunch exclaimed excitedly.

Her pretty mother smiled and said that Sunrise Beach was a good distance from Barham.

"It would take us almost a whole day to drive there by car," she told her small daughter.

Honey Bunch looked across the table at Flyer Frank.

"How long does it take you to go there in your plane?" she asked. "Can you get there in the wink of your eye?"

Flyer Frank laughed and so did Mr. and Mrs. Morton. They knew Honey Bunch was mixed up on two expressions the laundress, Mrs. Miller, used. One was "quick as a wink," and the other was "in the twinkling of an eye."

"My plane isn't that fast," the young man said, "but it's pretty fast. If I should leave here

26

now, I'd be in Sunrise Beach before you were asleep."

Honey Bunch giggled. She always stayed up later when Flyer Frank came, so he didn't know she usually went to bed right after dinner.

"Do you fly to Shell Horse Island in the plane you came here in?" the little girl asked.

The young man shook his head and said that this was his own plane, and too small to carry all the Island children.

"I use a Government plane when I fly to the Islands," he explained. "It carries more passengers and can land on the water."

Flyer Frank told the Mortons he collected about twenty children every morning, took them to Sunrise Beach and returned them after school.

Honey Bunch thought this must be the very nicest way to go to school. Imagine flying over the ocean every day!

All this time Daddy Morton had not said anything. Now he spoke up, looking first at his wife, then at his little daughter:

"I don't think I've ever mentioned it, but I have business in Sunrise Beach. I've been so busy here lately that I've put off taking care of it."

Honey Bunch got out of her chair and ran

around to her father. She put her arms around his neck, and looking straight at him, said:

"Oh, Daddy! You shouldn't put off the business any longer. Please take Mother and me to Sunrise Beach with you. I want to see the flying school children, and I want to see Flyer Frank's plane that can land on the water, and—if Flyer Frank will let me—maybe I can have a ride to the Islands."

Flyer Frank said he would make arrangements for her to go along on one of the trips. In the meantime, if her parents approved, he would take her up in his own plane this evening.

Then they went back to the airport and Honey Bunch had her little ride in the sky. It had been some time since her last trip over Barham at night. She loved the twinkling lights, especially the ones on moving cars.

There was only one thing the matter with the ride. It was over too soon! But when they landed at the airport, Honey Bunch was glad after all, because the first thing she saw was the dog Lucky.

"Oh, Daddy!" Honey Bunch cried. "He's the dog that saves everybody!" Mr. Morton had to go meet Dr. Hopewell and his famous collie. The pleasant young doctor asked if Mr. Reilly was all right. Honey Bunch said that he was.

"We left him home this time," she told the doctor. "I don't think we'll ever bring him to the airport again. He's a two-and-two dog."

"Whatever is that?" the doctor asked, smiling.

Honey Bunch was sorry she could not give the answer exactly. "It has something to do with getting into mischief," she said.

Honey Bunch and her parents watched as the doctor and Lucky took off to answer another call from a sick person on one of the Islands. Soon after, Flyer Frank, in his own plane, flew off and disappeared in the clouds.

"I hope so many things," said Honey Bunch with a sigh, as they walked back to the car.

"What are they?" her daddy asked.

"I hope we can go to Sunrise Beach, and I hope I can go up in Flyer Frank's plane that goes over the ocean, and I hope that Flyer Frank and Dr. Hopewell and Lucky don't have any trouble, and I hope . . ."

"And I hope my little girl will be able to sleep tonight." Mrs. Morton laughed. "This has been a pretty exciting evening for her."

Honey Bunch had no trouble sleeping, however. She did have one pleasant little dream in which she and Flyer Frank stopped at an island in the clouds and ate apple cake together. But this only made the night go faster.

When she woke up next morning, the sun was peeping through a window in her room. In a tree just outside, one bird was singing sweetly and several others were chattering gaily.

For a moment Honey Bunch lay still, listening to it all. Then, suddenly, she remembered that just before going to bed Daddy had promised to make a telephone call and find out if there would be room for them at the hotel in Sunrise Beach.

She got up quickly, put on her little robe and slippers, and hurried into the hall. Daddy and Mother's door was still closed. She must not awaken them.

The little girl was about to go back into her

own room when she heard a loud noise outdoors. The same shell whistle!

"Why, I thought Norman gave that to Flyer Frank," she said to herself.

Honey Bunch ran to the window and looked out. Then she called to her playmate, who was standing directly beneath the window.

"Norman, shush!" she said. "You'll wake everybody up."

"Nobody's asleep but you," he called up. "You're an old sleepyhead. It's nine o'clock!"

Honey Bunch was very much surprised. She never slept so late as this. She hurried into the hall again. Her mother was just coming up the stairs. She said that Daddy Morton already had left for his office.

"Little girls who sleep late miss their daddies," her mother said, laughing.

"But you know what he was going to tell me, don't you?" Honey Bunch asked her.

Mrs. Morton promised to tell the little girl all about it while she put on her clothes. Daddy Morton had made the telephone call and talked to the manager of the hotel at Sunrise Beach.

"Are we going?" Honey Bunch asked hopefully.

31

"Yes, dear. We'll leave tomorrow morning."

As soon as the little girl had eaten her breakfast, she ran outside to tell Norman where she was going. But first she inquired about the shell whistle.

"I thought you gave it to Flyer Frank," she said.

Norman hung his head. He said that when he tried to give Flyer Frank a lesson, the whistle had sort of broken. Since it did not work just right, he explained sheepishly, he could not give it away.

"But I fixed it," he added cheerfully.

Now that Honey Bunch was ready to tell Norman about her trip, she hesitated. Then suddenly she changed her mind and ran back into the house to ask her mother if Norman could go along.

Mrs. Morton was at the telephone and Honey Bunch could hardly believe her ears when she heard her mother say:

"It will be somebody for Honey Bunch to play with . . . yes, he's full of pep, but I'm sure he'll be good. . . . We'll leave about ten o'clock."

Mrs. Morton put down the telephone. Honey Bunch ran up to her.

"Mother, did I hear a secret?" she asked.

"Yes, you did, dear. But I was going to tell you about it. Norman will take the trip to Sunrise Beach with us."

"Oh goody!" Honey Bunch cried. "May I tell Norman now?"

Mrs. Morton said, "All right," and the little girl ran to the back yard. Norman was there with his whistle, and near him Mrs. Miller was hanging up laundry.

Just then Norman blew a loud blast on his whistle. The shell flew out of his mouth and hit the laundress on her arm.

"Oh!" she cried. "That does it! I can't take another minute of your noise!" With that she scooped up the whistle and the basket and stalked into the house. Norman looked glum.

"Never mind," said the little girl.

Honey Bunch now told him the big secret. The two children were going to Sunrise Beach on the ocean. They were going to start the very next morning, and it would take most all day to get there.

Norman let out a shout of glee that could be heard a block away. Then he picked up a stone from the driveway and pounded it on the steps of the back porch. Next he ran up and down the steps very fast, shouting wildly all the time.

Of course Mrs. Miller came outside. "You are the biggest nuisance I've ever seen," she said. "Your shell whistle is mild compared to this noise. Now take your whistle and go home!"

Honey Bunch felt like making some noise herself, so she followed Norman to his back yard. There they ran around playing airplane, sea gulls and waves on the ocean.

All that day the two children talked about the trip. They were up early the next morning, long before Daddy Morton was ready to start, and helped pack the car. Norman felt very important as he carried out the basket of lunch for the picnic they were to have on the way. Honey Bunch toted out two large thermos bottles.

"Good-bye, Mrs. Miller!" Honey Bunch cried out. "Please take good care of Mr. Reilly."

"I'll try," said the laundress.

At this moment she had Mr. Reilly by the collar. The pup was determined to get into the car and she was having all she could do to hold him back.

"I'm glad dogs don't cry," said Honey Bunch, "or I know Mr. Reilly would cry."

Lady Clare sat on the steps. The cat did not make so much fuss as the dog.

"Maybe it's because she's used to my going away so much," Honey Bunch thought. "When Mr. Reilly grows up maybe he'll be used to it, too."

Honey Bunch hoped that someday Mr. Reilly would be like Lucky. Of course, he would never look like him because Mr. Reilly was a police dog and Lucky was a collie. But the little girl hoped her dog would be as brave and help people the way Lucky did.

"I wonder if I'll ever see Lucky again," she thought, with a sigh.

The trip to Sunrise Beach seemed very long to Honey Bunch and Norman. At five o'clock they finally reached their destination. The hotel where they were going to stay was built right on the sand by the water.

Honey Bunch and Norman could hardly wait

to go out on the sand and play, but Mrs. Morton said it was too late that night. The next morning, however, they went out early. The first person they saw was an old fisherman strolling along the beach.

"Let's go and talk to him," Norman proposed.

The two children ran over to him and Honey Bunch asked how long he had lived there.

"All my life, little lass," he said. "But you've just come."

"How did you know?" Norman questioned.

"You haven't got the look of the sea in your eye yet," the old fisherman said, "and your skin's too white. The wind and the sun haven't tanned you yet."

"How long do you think it will take me to get the look of the sea in my eye?" Honey Bunch asked.

When she heard that it would take years, she laughed and said she could not stay there that long. They were only visiting and she and Norman wanted to find some shells in the sand.

"Do you have any special kind of shell here?" she asked the old fisherman.

"Yes, we do," he answered. "But you don't find one of them often. If you do find one, you can sell it for quite a little money."

"What's the name of it?" Honey Bunch asked.

"The Shell Horse. Years ago they used to find a lot of them out on Shell Horse Island. That's how the place got its name."

"How will we know a Shell Horse when we see it" Honey Bunch asked the old man.

"You'll know it right enough," he said, as he started to walk away. "The part where the opening is looks kind of like a horse's head."

Honey Bunch and Norman started digging as hard as they could. They did not see a boy about twelve years old coming up the beach.

Suddenly Norman exclaimed, "I've found one! I've found a Shell Horse!"

Quick as a wink the older boy dashed up to him and grabbed the shell from Norman's hand.

"It's mine!" he shouted. "You can't have it!"

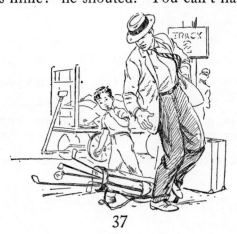

CHAPTER IV

THE MISSING SCHOOLBOY

"LET go!" Norman screamed at the top of his lungs.

The big boy paid no attention and started off with the Shell Horse.

Honey Bunch thought that this was very mean. Norman had found the shell and no one had a right to take it away from him. She grabbed hold of the big boy and cried out:

"You can't have it!"

"Who says I can't!" the boy answered, tugging to get away from the little girl and Norman. Both of them were holding his arms.

The old fisherman who had been talking to the children heard the cries. He hurried back to see what the trouble was. Honey Bunch and Norman quickly told him what the older boy was trying to do.

"The Shell Horse is mine!" the bigger boy insisted. "I buried it here."

The fisherman wanted to know if he could

prove this. To their surprise he replied that he could.

"I scratched this year's date on it," he said. "Here, look for yourself."

He handed the Shell Horse to the old man. Scratched on it were four numbers. The big boy repeated the numbers.

"You're right, son," said the fisherman, handing the shell back to him. "I guess it's yours. Where did you get it?"

"I found it."

Norman wanted to know why he had bothered to bury it. It was worth a lot of money. Why didn't he sell it?

The boy did not answer. Instead, he started to walk away. Honey Bunch ran after him.

"Do you live around here?" she asked.

"No, I live on one of the Islands."

"With a lighthouse?" Honey Bunch asked excitedly.

"Yes."

The big boy did not seem interested in talking to the children, but Honey Bunch and Norman walked alongside him just the same. They kept asking him one question after another.

"My, but you're nosy," the big boy said. "Where do you come from?"

Norman told him and then asked which island the older boy lived on. The boy said he lived on Shell Horse Island and his name was Steve Sampson.

"Go on now and leave me alone," he said, annoyed, and gave Norman a shove.

Norman tumbled over onto the sand. Honey Bunch decided she did not like the big boy.

"Come on, Norman," she said as he got up. "Let's hunt for another Shell Horse."

The two children hunted all morning until it was time to go swimming. In fact, while they were playing in the waves, Norman kept digging his toes into the sand, hoping to find another rare shell. He and Honey Bunch picked

up many pretty ones but did not come across any shells more than an inch long.

When they returned to the beach after lunch, Honey Bunch noticed the old fisherman standing on the shore, holding a long rod. She told Norman, and the two children ran over to watch him.

Attached to the rod was the longest fishing line Honey Bunch had ever seen. As they watched, the man turned a little wheel on the side of the rod and pulled the line in.

"Aw, shucks," said Norman. "There's no fish on it."

By this time the children had reached the old man's side. He took a small clam from a basket on the sand and attached it to a hook on the end of the line. Then, holding the handle of the rod tightly in both hands, he swung it first backward, then forward. The little clam went whizzing through the air on the end of the line, away out over the waves.

The old fisherman stood very still and did not say a word. So Honey Bunch and Norman did the same, although Honey Bunch did not see any need for being so quiet when the waves were making so much noise.

41

"But maybe when you're quiet as a mouse," Honey Bunch thought, using one of Mrs. Miller's pet expressions, "you'll catch a big fish."

The little girl seemed to have guessed right. In about three minutes, when she and Norman were sure they could not keep quiet any longer, the old fisherman felt a strong tug on his line.

"Guess I've got a lallapaloosa," he said.

"What kind of fish is that?" Norman wanted to know.

The old man laughed and said that was not the name of a fish, it just meant something very, very big. Honey Bunch decided at once that she must tell Mrs. Miller about this. She was sure the laundress did not know the word.

"Here he comes!" the old fisherman cried in delight, reeling in his line a little at a time.

Presently, up from the waves leaped a great big sea bass. It disappeared in the water again, and kept turning and twisting very fast until it was finally pulled to shore. There it flopped around on the sand.

"Is he really a lallapaloosa?" Honey Bunch wanted to know.

"He sure is," the old fisherman said. "That bass must weigh all of fifteen pounds!"

"Will you get a lot of money for him?" Norman asked.

"I reckon so," the fisherman replied. "How'd you like some nice fresh sea bass for dinner?"

Honey Bunch had never thought of eating the fish, but she liked sea bass.

"I think I'll sell it to the hotel," the man told the children. "It will be served tonight."

"Do you work for the hotel?" Honey Bunch inquired.

The old man said he worked for everybody. He earned his living catching fish and selling them to anybody who wanted to buy them. But when he caught a lallapaloosa, he always sold it to the hotel.

Honey Bunch heard her name called and turned to see her mother coming toward them. She had been sitting on the sand farther down the beach, watching them play.

She said if they wanted to go meet Flyer Frank they would have to hurry. It had been arranged that Honey Bunch and Norman would go to the school which the Island children attended and watch them take off in Flyer Frank's plane for their homes.

Honey Bunch and Norman said good-bye to

43

the fisherman and ran to meet Mrs. Morton.

They drove into the town of Sunrise Beach and parked. Mrs. Morton suggested that the children go into a gift shop near the car. She would come for them in a few minutes.

Honey Bunch hurried inside the store, followed by Norman. A gleaming white dollhouse stood on a table in the center of the floor. It was made of beautiful shells of many colors.

"Doesn't anybody live in the dollhouse?" Honey Bunch asked the shopkeeper.

"Oh, yes. Just peek in the windows and see," the man suggested.

Honey Bunch looked through the living-room

window. Several dolls sat on the chairs. One was seated at a tiny piano made of shells.

The dolls themselves were made from shells also, but they were dressed in clothes made from pieces of silk.

"They're having a party!" Honey Bunch cried.

"That's right." The man smiled. "Listen carefully."

All of a sudden the tiny figure at the piano began to play, and lovely, tinkling music sounded. Norman, who had thought he was not interested in dolls and dollhouses, came running back from the other side of the store.

He could not figure out how the little doll could possibly play the piano. Neither could Honey Bunch.

Finally the man showed them. There was a little music box in back of the dollhouse, which he had wound up.

Norman asked the man how much the dollhouse cost.

"Oh, it isn't for sale," the shopkeeper replied. "It took me ten years to build this."

"Ten years!" Honey Bunch gasped. "Why, you started to make the dollhouse before I was even a little teeny, tiny baby!"

"Why did it take so long?" Norman asked.

The man said he could work on the dollhouse only in his spare time. Furthermore, he had had to gather all the shells before starting to build it.

"You wouldn't believe it," he said, "but it took thousands and thousands of shells to make the house, the furniture and the dolls."

"Oh," gasped Honey Bunch, "and did you gather all of them yourself?"

"Yes, every one," the man said proudly.

Honey Bunch said that she was going to collect enough pretty shells so that someday she might have a dollhouse as beautiful as this one. Norman remarked that this would be a waste of time. He would rather hunt for a Shell Horse and sell it.

"Oh, you've heard about the Shell Horses," the man remarked.

Norman told him how he had found one on the beach that morning but had had to give it up. The shopkeeper told Norman if he ever did find another one to bring it to the store.

Mrs. Morton came for the children at this moment and hurried off with them to the school. In front of it stood a large bus marked SCHOOL BUS. Flyer Frank was not in sight, but he arrived in a few minutes.

46

"Hello, everybody," he said.

He explained that usually he did not come to the school for the children. The bus brought them to the airport.

"But I thought maybe you'd like to meet the children here," he said, "and ride out in the bus with them."

"Oh, that'll be fun," said Honey Bunch.

In a few minutes several children came out of the large, brick school building. None of them came toward the bus. Finally Honey Bunch inquired what the trouble was.

Flyer Frank smiled. "They're not Island children," he said. "My children will be here in a few minutes. They like to play around after school a little while. We'll probably find them in the yard."

He took Honey Bunch and Norman around to the rear of the building. Several boys and girls were playing on swings and "skinning-the-cat" on a metal bar.

"Are these your Island children?" Honey Bunch asked.

"Most of them," Flyer Frank replied.

"Is Steve Sampson here?" Norman wanted to know. "I don't like him."

Flyer Frank asked how in the world Norman

Clark knew Steve Sampson and why he did not like him. Norman soon told him.

"That sounds like Steve," the young man said.

Steve was not in the yard, but several of the other children ran up to Flyer Frank and were introduced to Honey Bunch and Norman.

Honey Bunch particularly liked one little girl about a year older than herself whose name was Priscilla. Honey Bunch was surprised to hear that the little girl was Steve's sister.

"You live on Shell Horse Island, don't you?" she said to Priscilla.

"Yes, I do."

"I do, too," said a little boy, "and it's the best lighthouse on the coast!"

"It is not," shouted another boy. "Ours is!"

At this point Flyer Frank stepped in. "Every lighthouse island is very fine," he said, "and

every one is very useful. Each of you children should be proud to be part of a great service to your country. Come on now, we'll get in the bus."

He led the way to the street. Four children already were seated in the bus. The others climbed in, and then Flyer Frank counted noses.

With Norman and Honey Bunch there should have been twenty-two children. But there were only twenty-one.

"Somebody's missing," said Flyer Frank. "Who is it?"

There was a buzz of voices. Finally someone said that it was Steve Sampson who was missing. His sister Priscilla was sent back into the school to find him. In a few minutes she came out to report that he was not there.

"Where can my brother be?" she asked with a little catch in her voice.

Honey Bunch put her arm around the other little girl's shoulder. "Maybe he's on the beach," she said.

Flyer Frank went into the school to use the telephone. He called the old fisherman, who lived right on the seashore.

When Flyer Frank came back he said the old man had gone out on his porch and looked up and down the beach but had not spotted Steve Sampson anywhere.

The young man became worried. He told Mrs. Morton he felt a personal responsibility for the children. This was the first time one of them had been missing.

"We can't go without him," the pilot said. "Something may have happened to him. Steve is the kind of boy who often gets into mischief."

Honey Bunch had been sitting quietly, thinking very hard. Mrs. Miller had once told her when she wanted to find out something, to "put on her thinking cap." So that was just what Honey Bunch was doing. Of course, she didn't really have a cap. But she put her hands on her head, which made it feel as if she were wearing a little hat. Suddenly she exclaimed:

"Flyer Frank, I think I know where Steve Sampson is!"

CHAPTER V

THE FLYING BOAT

EVERYONE looked at Honey Bunch, wondering how she could possibly know where the boy was.

"I believe," said Honey Bunch slowly, "that Steve is at the dollhouse store."

"What is that?" Flyer Frank asked, puzzled.

"Oh, I know," said Steve's sister Priscilla. "It's a gift shop in town. But Steve wouldn't have any reason for going there."

Honey Bunch told Flyer Frank why she thought they might find the big boy at the shop. He might be trying to sell the Shell Horse Norman had dug up out of the sand.

Priscilla looked surprised. She had not known her brother had found one of the rare shells. Suddenly she giggled.

"Maybe that's what the lump was under his sweater this morning," she said. "I thought it was his sandwiches."

All the children in the bus laughed. They re-

membered about the lump under Steve's sweater
and how Steve would not tell what it was. One
of the boys said that Steve had asked him for a
sandwich at lunchtime. Probably Steve had
brought the Shell Horse from the Island in his
sandwich bag.

"Mrs. Morton," said Flyer Frank, "may I
borrow your car and run downtown to see if I
can find Steve?"

"Yes, indeed. Here's the key."

The young pilot hurried off. While the children waited for him to return, Priscilla and
Honey Bunch sat down in one of the double
seats of the bus. Priscilla whispered to her new
friend that she was very much worried about
her brother.

"You think he's run away?" Honey Bunch
asked.

"Maybe," the other little girl replied, "but
I don't think so."

She went on to say that Steve had been late
for school that morning. He must have gone off
to bury the rare shell.

"My daddy," said Priscilla, "has a collection
of sea shells that lots of people come to see. But
he hasn't any Shell Horse in it. He told us that
if we ever found one he would like to have it."

"You mean," said Honey Bunch, "that Steve found one and didn't give it to your daddy?"

Priscilla nodded. "Daddy will scold Steve if he ever finds out," she said.

In a few minutes the Morton car came back. In it were Flyer Frank and Steve Sampson. As the boy walked into the bus, the other children began asking him questions. One boy said, "Teacher caught you!" And one little girl snickered as he went by.

Steve turned red. "You kids keep still or I'll punch you!" he threatened. "I guess I've got a right to go where I want!"

Suddenly he saw Honey Bunch seated beside his sister. He pulled her out of the seat.

"You're to blame for this," he said. "Get out of here and mind your own business!"

Mrs. Morton jumped from her seat to Honey

Bunch's side. At the same moment Flyer Frank grabbed Steve Sampson.

"See here, young man!" he cried. "You stop such talk or you'll really get into trouble. Now get in that seat up front and don't make another sound!"

The children had never heard Flyer Frank speak like this, and a hush fell over the bus. Steve was the most surprised of all and got to his seat in a hurry.

Flyer Frank gave the bus driver the go-ahead signal, and they started for the airport. Priscilla continued to tell Honey Bunch what a nice place Shell Horse Island was.

"I'll tell Mother and Daddy not to let Steve bother you and Norman if you come," she whispered.

Flyer Frank walked toward the rear of the bus to speak to Mrs. Morton. On the way Honey Bunch grabbed hold of his hand.

"I don't want to be a box of questions," she said, twisting around an expression Mrs. Miller used for Norman when she called him a question box. "But am I going to Shell Horse Island with you sometime?"

"Sooner than you think," he answered, smiling.

"When?"

"Tomorrow afternoon," Flyer Frank replied. "On Saturdays I always deliver meat and groceries to all the islands."

Honey Bunch was thrilled. She was so excited that she jumped up into the aisle.

"Norman, did you hear that!" she cried. "We're going in Flyer Frank's plane tomorrow!"

Steve Sampson, who had kept quiet for a few minutes, turned around. "What's so wonderful about that?" he said. "I go in it every day."

But Honey Bunch and Norman were not going to let Steve spoil their good time. It was only because the bus gave a lurch and Honey Bunch was suddenly thrown into her seat that she sat down. She felt more like dancing and skipping around.

"Oh, I'm so glad," said Priscilla. She looked up at the pilot and added, "Mr. Franklin, won't you stay a long time at Shell Horse, so Honey Bunch and I can play together?"

It seemed funny to Honey Bunch to hear the young man called Mr. Franklin. It had been a long time since she had heard the pilot's last name. She told Priscilla that she always called him Flyer Frank.

"I like that name better for you, Mr. Franklin," said the Island girl. "May I call you that too?"

"I like it better myself." Flyer Frank smiled, and said, "How about all you children calling me that?"

Every child in the bus was enthusiastic about the idea except Steve. He grunted some kind of reply. Honey Bunch could not hear him very well, but it sounded like "You'd think there weren't any other flyers in the world."

Honey Bunch thought Steve was about the rudest boy she had ever met. She did not think any more about him for the moment, however, because the bus had reached the airport. Everyone got out and the Island children ran toward Flyer Frank's school plane. Honey Bunch and Norman followed with the pilot.

The little girl had expected that the plane would be resting on the water. She was surprised to see it standing on wheels on the ground.

"How do you land on the water?" she asked.

Flyer Frank explained that after he got his plane into the air, he pulled the wheels up tight underneath it.

"If you will look closely," he said, "you will notice the bottom of the plane is like a boat."

Secretly Honey Bunch and Norman wished they might go along with the other children. The weather was just right for flying. The next day might be stormy, and then Mrs. Morton would not let them go. But there was not room for them in the plane.

"See you tomorrow," Flyer Frank called gaily, as he ran up the ladder after the children and went through the doorway.

The door swung shut. A moment later the two motors roared. The plane raced down the runway and glided up into the sky like a big sea gull.

As the bus driver took Mrs. Morton and the children back to pick up their car, Honey Bunch and Norman could talk of nothing but their coming trip. The evening seemed to drag. The next morning on the beach did not seem to be so much fun as it had been the day before. Wouldn't afternoon ever come?

Then something interesting happened. Daddy Morton, who had not seen much of his family since arriving at Sunrise Beach, came to play with the children on the sand. In his hand he carried a large, mechanical toy.

When it was wound up, six little buckets attached to a chain began to move. They scooped

57

up sand and dumped it into a little red truck.

"Oh, I want to make it go!" cried Norman.

He wound it up. As the first bucket threw off its load, the little boy gasped. A candy, wrapped in paper, had landed in the truck.

"See what I dug up!" Norman exclaimed. "It's mine!"

He watched eagerly to see if anything more came from the sand before the machine stopped, but nothing did.

"It's my turn," said Honey Bunch.

She did not expect to be so lucky as Norman. But to her surprise she also dug up a caramel.

"Well, this is a lucky shovel," Mr. Morton said, laughing.

Honey Bunch and Norman wished they might dig up a Shell Horse, but of course it would be too large for the bucket to hold.

Norman set the machine in a different spot and wound it up again. He watched carefully. There was a plopping sound in the truck.

"I've got something!" he cried.

A tiny toy automobile gleamed in the sun.

"Oh, boy! Am I lucky!" the little boy shouted. "People drop all sorts of things on beaches, don't they, Mr. Morton?"

Honey Bunch's daddy merely smiled. He told

Honey Bunch to wind up the red truck again.

"I hope I get a surprise too," she said.

Quickly she set the toy going and, sure enough, a little box dropped into the truck. Inside it was a tiny ring with a blue stone in it.

"Oh, it's pretty, Daddy!" the little girl exclaimed.

She noticed that there seemed to be a special twinkle in his eyes. Then he winked at her, and Honey Bunch caught on. Daddy had buried the gifts in the sand!

"Thank you," she said, winking back. She was sure the next treasure would be something unusual. But she was amazed to see what landed in the truck. Six tiny crabs.

"Oh!" cried the little girl. "Look out! They'll pinch you, Norman!"

Then suddenly Honey Bunch laughed. She remembered that baby crabs were not like the

59

big crabs one eats. They did not pinch like their big relatives.

But at that very moment she saw something that made her cry out. Right behind Daddy crawled a huge pinching crab. In another instant it would certainly pinch her daddy!

"Daddy! Look out!" she cried.

Mr. Morton moved just in time. Honey Bunch and Norman jumped up, too. Then, right where Mr. Morton had been sitting, the crab burrowed down into the sand and disappeared.

"Hm," said Daddy Morton, "I guess the joke's on me after all. That must have been the mother crab. She was probably looking for her babies."

As he said this, Norman gazed at him, a funny look on his face. Suddenly it dawned on him that Mr. Morton had put the candy and the automobile in the sand, so the children could scoop them up. The boy laughed good-naturedly.

A few minutes later, when the three of them got back to the hotel, he spied Flyer Frank in a corner of the lobby, talking to Mrs. Morton.

"He's here!" Norman shouted. "First one to Flyer Frank gets to sit alongside of him in the plane!"

Mr. Morton laughed and stopped the little boy as he started to dash across the lobby. "Wait a minute, Norman. You and Honey Bunch will both get a chance to sit with Flyer Frank if you behave yourselves."

Norman promised to be good. Indeed, he was very good during the ride to the airport and even after the two children climbed into the plane.

"We'll be back in about two hours," Flyer Frank called, as he strapped the children's seat belts.

"Mr. Morton and I will be waiting for you here," said Honey Bunch's mother.

The two children waved as long as they could see Honey Bunch's parents on the ground. Presently they were passing over the buildings of Sunrise Beach, the schoolhouse, the gift shop, the hotel. Now they were out over the water.

"This is really an air boat, isn't it?" Honey Bunch asked Flyer Frank.

"That's a good name for it, Honey Bunch," the pilot said, smiling, "but it's called a flying boat. And now look ahead, children. In a minute you'll see the first island where we're going to stop."

"Does it have a lighthouse on it?" Honey Bunch wanted to know.

"Oh, yes," Flyer Frank replied. "All the islands where we'll stop have lighthouses. And

61

they have pretty names, too. The one we're coming to is called Pearl Lighthouse. That's because one of the biggest pearls ever found was picked up in an oyster shell on the beach there."

Soon the children could see the lighthouse in the distance. In a very few minutes Flyer Frank set his flying boat down on the water near a small dock.

A boy and a girl came running down to the dock to greet them. Honey Bunch recognized them from the day before.

Flyer Frank and the children's father, who came alongside the plane in a rowboat, unloaded boxes and crates of food from the flying boat in a very short time.

"Sorry we can't stay longer," said Flyer Frank, "but we must visit the other islands too."

"What will you do when you don't have to fly

your children to school any more?" Honey Bunch asked.

The young man laughed. "Then I'll fly the summer people back and forth. They like to come by plane instead of by boat."

One by one the Lighthouse Islands were visited. Finally only Shell Horse Island was left.

"That's the farthest one out in the ocean," said Flyer Frank. "It's quite a little ride from here. Keep your eyes open. See which one of you can find it first."

As Honey Bunch and Norman were staring down over the water, all of a sudden one of the flying boat's motors made a funny noise. It sounded like somebody trying to cough.

Honey Bunch looked at Flyer Frank. A worried frown had come over his face.

"Are we in trouble?" the little girl asked. She had once heard Mother ask Daddy that question when their automobile engine had coughed in very much the same way.

Flyer Frank did not reply. At this moment the motor went dead.

The pilot wondered whether he could get himself and the children safely down on the water before the other motor died too!

CHAPTER VI

THE LIGHTHOUSE

IT WAS not necessary for Flyer Frank to answer Honey Bunch's question. She knew the flying boat was in trouble.

The pilot leaned forward and turned several knobs on the dashboard of his plane. Then he picked up what looked like a telephone and said:

"Calling Shell Horse Island. Franklin coming in. One motor dead."

Honey Bunch and Norman held their breaths. Up to this moment the ride in the big flying boat had been fun. Now they did not know what was going to happen.

"Calling Shell Horse Island," said Flyer Frank again.

Honey Bunch and Norman sat very still in their seats and looked out the windows. They could see Shell Horse Island in the distance, but below them was nothing but water. They realized the flying boat was getting nearer and nearer to it every second. Both of them wondered just when they would hit the water and what would happen next.

Then, all of a sudden, they were skimming along the top of the waves. They felt only a little slap, slap, slap on the bottom of the plane. The flying boat went whizzing along for about half a minute. Then it slowed down and presently stopped.

"Whew!" exclaimed Flyer Frank. "I wasn't sure I could do it!"

Honey Bunch got out of her seat and ran up to the pilot. She gave him a big hug.

"Oh, Flyer Frank, you're a wise-old-owl flying man!" she said.

The pilot laughed and relaxed. It was the best thing anyone could have said to him at that moment.

"I hope I'll always be a wise old owl in the air," he chuckled, "especially when you're with me."

To the children's surprise, they were right near Shell Horse Island. When Flyer Frank opened the door, they saw land and rocks and several people. The Island folks had heard Flyer Frank's call over the radio. Mr. Sampson, the lightkeeper, had picked up the message and hurried out in his motorboat to where Flyer Frank usually landed on the water.

"Thank goodness you made it!" he said. "Priscilla here was with me when the message came. She was beside herself with worry."

Honey Bunch and Norman guessed that the tall, thin man was Priscilla and Steve's father.

Flyer Frank already was examining the motor that had gone dead. Now he shook his head.

"I'm afraid you have some visitors on your hands," he said to Mr. Sampson. "I'll need a new part for this motor before I can fly again, and there's not a chance of getting it before Monday morning."

Mr. Sampson said he and Mrs. Sampson would be delighted to have Flyer Frank and the children as their guests.

"We may be a little crowded," he said, "but I guess you won't mind. There'll be plenty of food. Good thing the supplies didn't drop in the ocean, Frank."

Norman thought so, too. Already he was becoming hungry. He thought it would be fun to stay on the Island. This was the first time in his life and Honey Bunch's, too, that they had been so far away from home without either Mr. and Mrs. Morton, or Mr. and Mrs. Clark.

A sudden thought struck Honey Bunch.

"We didn't bring any clothes," she said.

"I'll lend you some," Priscilla offered.

"How about me?" said Norman. Then he thought of something. "When a sailor gets shipwrecked on an island, he doesn't need any clothes. I'm going to be a shipwrecked sailor until Monday."

As they started up the hill Honey Bunch looked all around. She did not want to miss a single thing on Shell Horse Island.

This side of the Island had a small dock and was rather sandy. But the rest of the shore line was rocky. To get to the lighthouse one had to walk up a rather steep hill. The lighthouse was at the top of it, a good distance above the ocean.

On the way up to it, Honey Bunch saw two

houses. Priscilla told her two other families lived in them. Their children had gone off in a boat to the mainland but would be back in a little while.

Next they came to a barn. Honey Bunch wondered why anyone would have a barn away out here on the ocean. She soon found out. In the barn stood several cows.

"We have to have fresh milk for our children," explained Lightkeeper Sampson. "Sometimes when we have bad storms here, nobody can land to bring us food."

"Oh, how dreadful!" said Honey Bunch.

"We don't mind too much, do we, Priscilla?" Her father smiled. "We usually have enough to eat. What concern us more are the ships and planes at sea that get into trouble during storms."

"But you always keep your light burning for them, don't you?"

"Of course," Mr. Sampson replied. "We have two systems here to keep the big lamp lighted. We make our own electricity. If that goes bad, we use oil. That's the oil house over there."

They walked on, and Norman asked what the next building was. Lightkeeper Sampson said he would show them. He went inside and suddenly the air was filled with a terrific noise.

Honey Bunch decided it was ten thousand times louder than Norman's shell whistle, and sounded like giant cows crying.

"What is it?" she asked Priscilla.

"That's in case of fog," the Island girl replied. "When the fog gets so bad that it's hard to see the light, Daddy turns on the fog signal."

"I guess the people on the boats don't have any trouble hearing it," said Honey Bunch.

All this time they had been getting nearer and nearer the lighthouse itself. It was so big that Honey Bunch felt like a little ant looking up at the building. It was perfectly round and reached a height of about a hundred feet in the air.

Next to it was the little house where the Sampson family lived. It was very pretty with its green shutters and window boxes full of flowers.

"We'll go in here first," said the lightkeeper.

"and meet my wife. She'll be a little surprised to hear about her sudden company, but I know she'll be glad to have you."

Honey Bunch hoped so. What would they do if she did not want to keep them? But Mrs. Sampson proved to be a lovely, motherly person. She was sorry to hear about the trouble Flyer Frank had had with his flying boat.

"I'm very glad to have you stay," she said, "and I know Priscilla is glad, too. Now she'll have a lovely little girl to play with."

"And a boy, too," Norman spoke up.

Mrs. Sampson said she was sure Norman was a nice boy and that he would enjoy playing with her son Steve.

"Oh, no, I won't," Norman said bluntly.

Mrs. Sampson looked surprised. "How do you know?" she asked.

Priscilla spoke up. She told her mother she had not wanted to tattle on her brother, but he had not been very nice to either Honey Bunch or Norman at Sunrise Beach.

"Where is Steve?" she asked suddenly.

"He went off in the boat with the other children," her mother replied.

Secretly, Norman wished he would stay away for the whole week end, but he was not to have his wish granted. Steve returned before Honey Bunch and Norman had even had a chance to see the inside of the lighthouse. When the big boy heard the visitors would be there and that Norman would share his bedroom, until Monday, he scowled.

"I don't want that fresh kid in my bedroom," he said, and looked straight at Norman.

"Why, Steve Sampson," his mother said. "Don't talk like that! Of course Norman will share your bedroom with you."

But Norman did not like the idea either. Steve was bigger than he was, and Norman remembered how the other boy had shoved him, down on the beach. Suddenly Norman thought he had a bright idea.

"Mrs. Sampson, why don't you let Flyer Frank sleep with Steve?" he suggested. "I can sleep on your living-room couch."

The pilot of the flying boat smiled. "No, Norman," he said. "I'm too big for Steve's bed."

Then Mrs. Sampson added, "If Steve is naughty, Norman, you let Flyer Frank know. You see, his couch is right by the door to Steve's bedroom."

Hearing this, Norman felt better about the arrangement. In the meantime, Priscilla had

71

taken Honey Bunch to her room and shown the visitor her dolls and other toys.

"Honey Bunch!" Flyer Frank called. "I radioed your mother and father and told them we're staying here until Monday. And now, do you want to see the lighthouse?"

Honey Bunch ran from the bedroom and followed the others to the inside of the tall tower. Near the wall was a narrow, iron staircase with a hand rail on one side. It wound round and round as it went to the top of the lighthouse.

Finally, up where the big light was, they came to a wooden footway with a railing, which went all the way around the light.

"But where is the light?" Norman asked, as they reached the top. He could see nothing but several large, green cloths.

"The light is under the cloths," Mr. Sampson explained. "Over the light itself are many, many pieces of glass. In the daytime, when the sun is shining, there is a great reflection from the glass."

"But why do you cover them up?" Norman asked.

"Because," said the lightkeeper, "the reflection is so strong it would bother the captain of a ship and all the people on it."

Honey Bunch and Norman knew what Mr. Sampson meant. They sometimes played a game with a little mirror. They would let the sun shine down on it and then move the mirror around, so that the reflected light would hit some person or object.

"When will you take the green cloths off?" Honey Bunch wanted to know.

"About sundown," the lightkeeper replied. "Would you like to come up with me when I turn the light on?"

"Oh, yes," said Honey Bunch and Norman together.

The children played in the tower for a while, then Mrs. Sampson called them to supper. It really was supper, not dinner, as Honey Bunch was used to in the evening. But that was because

73

Mr. Sampson was home all the time, and they had dinner in the middle of the day.

"Time to go upstairs," said Lightkeeper Sampson, rising from the table later on.

The children followed him up the winding stairway. First he climbed a little ladder and carefully folded back one of the green curtains. After folding it up, he took off another. There were four altogether.

Next he turned a big wheel. Slowly, the many glasses which covered the light began to go round and round in a circle. Honey Bunch saw something she had not noticed before. The top of the lighthouse had windows all the way around. They were very tall windows; in fact, almost as high as a room.

Next, Mr. Sampson clicked a switch. In a moment the light began to burn.

"Now you had better go downstairs," the lightkeeper said. "The light will hurt your eyes if you stay here."

As the children went down the winding stairway, they knew what he meant. The place grew brighter and brighter.

Hurrying outside, Honey Bunch and Norman ran off to a little distance to look up at the light. It was very, very bright, indeed.

"Doesn't it ever get dark?" Honey Bunch asked Priscilla.

"Well, when we have a bad storm it seems darker. You know," she added, "I'm afraid we may have a storm tonight."

"How can you tell?" Honey Bunch wanted to know.

Priscilla was such a little girl that Honey Bunch wondered how she could possibly know. The weather seemed very clear and nice right now.

"I've listened to Daddy talk about weather signs so many times, I can just feel it," Priscilla answered.

Finally the children went into the house. Mrs. Sampson had the radio on. Honey Bunch did not pay much attention to it at first, but suddenly a name came to her ears that made her listen carefully.

"In spite of bad weather reports, the famous dog Lucky and his master have just taken off on another long trip," the announcer was saying. "Dr. Hopewell and his pal are flying to a sick child up North to take her some rare medicine that reached the doctor at the Barham airport less than an hour ago."

As the announcer went on to other news items,

Honey Bunch cried out, "Oh, Priscilla, they were in Barham, where I live, the other day. Lucky is the most beautiful dog you ever saw. He's a lifesaving dog."

Since Mrs. Sampson and Priscilla had never heard about him, Honey Bunch told them the story. When she finished, Mrs. Sampson remarked:

"That is a wonderful combination: a doctor that saves lives, and a dog that saves lives."

"I'd like to see them sometime," said Priscilla.

Before the children went to bed, the wind began to blow very hard.

Priscilla had been right. The weather was getting rough.

It soon grew so bad that windows and doors had to be closed tightly. Honey Bunch lay in bed, next to Priscilla, wide awake. Even the little Island girl, who was used to shrieking wind, could not sleep, either.

"We're going to have a very dreadful storm," she said finally. "I don't like storms."

"Why?" Honey Bunch asked.

"Because we never know," Priscilla answered, "when one of them is going to be a hurricane. It might even blow everything right off the Island!"

CHAPTER VII

THE HURRICANE

IN ANOTHER bedroom Norman Clark and Steve Sampson lay talking about the storm. Steve knew a great deal about hurricanes and he frightened the little boy so much that Norman came running out into the living room.

"Flyer Frank! Flyer Frank!" he cried. "Where are you?"

The pilot was stretched out on a couch, but he was awake.

"Couldn't you sleep, little man?" he said.

Norman was sobbing. "Waves are going to go right over the Island," he cried. "All the buildings are going to blow away. Please, Flyer Frank, take me home!"

The young man put his arm around the little boy's shoulders and tried to comfort him. Secretly, the pilot was fearful that his plane would be torn away from its moorings and lost.

Suddenly the door to another bedroom opened. Out came Honey Bunch and Priscilla. They looked very cute in their long, flowered nighties trimmed with ruffles. The little girls were frightened, too.

"I'm going to get Daddy and Mother," said Priscilla. "We ought to go into the tower."

She explained that whenever they had an unusually bad storm, everyone on the Island gathered inside the lighthouse. It was built on solid rock and would be the one thing on the Island which could not blow away.

"Th—then let's go in it," wailed Norman.

Before Priscilla had a chance to go for her parents, they came into the room. Both were fully dressed. They told Honey Bunch and Priscilla to put on their clothes quickly. Then Mr. Sampson went into Steve's room and told him to dress also.

In about five minutes the whole group was ushered through an iron doorway into the base of the big lighthouse. Honey Bunch felt better right away. The wind did not seem so loud here, and the big light up above beamed steadily. It seemed very friendly and comforting.

It had the same effect on Norman Clark. He stopped crying and asked Mr. Sampson if he might go up the spiral stairway and look out the window at the storm.

"Go ahead," the lightkeeper replied. "Why don't all you children go up there?"

Steve did not consider himself a child, so he remained below. The other children scrambled up the iron stairs to the platform and looked out.

"I can't see anything," said Norman in disappointment.

The reason was that the wind was blowing the spray from the ocean against the glass.

"Does the spray cover the windows by the light?" Norman asked Priscilla.

"Sure."

"Can the light shine through it?" the little boy wanted to know.

"Of course," said Priscilla. "That's when the ships' captains need it most—in a storm."

The storm was now raging furiously. Mr. Sampson went to a telephone on the wall.

"What's he going to do now?" Norman asked, looking down over the edge of the platform.

"I guess he's going to tell the other people on the Island to come here," said Priscilla.

But as her father picked up the telephone, one of the iron doors opened, and two men and their wives and four children staggered in. Their clothes were ripped and their hair was straggling in every direction.

"I thought we'd never get here," said one of the women, gasping for breath.

A man was trying to close the door, but the wind was so strong he could not do it alone.

"Give—me a—hand!" he called out.

Mr. Sampson and Flyer Frank rushed to help him. It took the combined strength of the three men to push the door shut and bolt it.

"This is the worst storm we've had since I came here to work," said one of the men who had just come in. "It's a regular hurricane."

Honey Bunch and Norman began to feel frightened all over again. But they felt better when Lightkeeper Sampson said:

"Let the wind blow! Nothing can happen to this faithful old lighthouse!"

Within a few minutes the rain began to fall in torrents.

The Hurricane

The little girl thought about the ships out on the ocean. What were the wind and the rain and the waves doing to them? Could their captains see the big light above her and steer away from the dangerous rocks?

Suddenly the little girl thought of Dr. Hopewell and his lovely dog Lucky. Were they safe? Or had the doctor's plane been caught in the storm?

She was about to come down the stairway to ask if the storm was blowing over the land too, when suddenly the big light went out!

"Oh!" cried Honey Bunch.

"Quick!" she heard Lightkeeper Sampson say. "The oil pump, men!"

In the darkness, Honey Bunch could hear scuffling. A moment later a flashlight shone. Then a large searchlight was turned on. A trap door in the floor was raised and two men went down a ladder. Lightkeeper Sampson himself hurried up the spiral staircase. In a very few minutes the big light once more was shining out through the storm.

Just how many hours Honey Bunch and the others stayed in the tower the little girl did not know. The continuous roaring of the wind and the beating of the rain on the roof gradually lulled her to sleep. The next thing Honey Bunch knew, she was waking up back in the bed beside Priscilla.

The storm was over!

"This house didn't blow away," Honey Bunch thought thankfully. "I wonder about the other people. And the cows. Oh, I hope they're all right!"

Priscilla was still asleep, so Honey Bunch got up very quietly and began to dress. Suddenly she heard strange squawkings outside.

"It sounds like a hundred cars tooting their horns," Honey Bunch giggled.

She quickly put on her dress and tiptoed out to the living room. Flyer Frank was just waking up. He yawned and stretched his arms as he opened his eyes.

"Why, good morning, Honey Bunch," he said. "Well, we rode out the storm all right."

"Is our flying boat all right?" the little girl asked quickly.

"Yes, she's still there," the young man replied. "I expect she's full of water, though."

He told Honey Bunch that she and the other children had been carried back to their beds sound asleep. He and the other grownups had not gone to bed until the storm had ended and

82

then they had made a tour of the Island. Two sheds had blown down and part of the barn roof had been ripped off.

"But the cows are safe and we'll have fresh milk for breakfast," he said, smiling.

Again the strange honking sounded outside. Honey Bunch asked the flyer if he knew what it was.

"I think the wild ducks are tuning up," he answered. "Let's go see."

They went outside. It was a gray, misty morning. Flying around the lighthouse were large and small ducks. Every once in a while they would come down to rest either on the water or on the Island.

"Are they trying to find something to eat?" Honey Bunch asked.

"They sure are," Flyer Frank replied. "They're probably on the way to the mainland but stopped here to see what they could find."

"Let's feed them," Honey Bunch suggested, and added, "Oh, aren't the babies cute? I wish I could have one."

"I'll see what I can do for you," said Flyer Frank.

He led her to the kitchen of the Sampson house, where they found a small bag of corn.

They brought it outside, and Flyer Frank made a noise that sounded just like Daddy Morton's automobile horn.

"Now throw some corn on the ground," he instructed.

Honey Bunch did this, and in a moment a young duck flew down to gobble up the kernels. Flyer Frank grabbed the soft, downy bird and held it firmly in his hands. Honey Bunch fed it some corn from the palm of her hand and stroked its head and back.

All of a sudden there was a great racket and a duck came flying toward them.

"Oh, oh," said the young man. "Here comes the baby's mother!"

"Is she angry?" Honey Bunch shouted above the loud, honking noise the big duck was making.

"Yes, I think she is. She doesn't understand

that we are just admiring her baby. She's afraid we're hurting it."

"Well, if I tell her we like her baby, will she go away?" asked Honey Bunch.

"No, I'm afraid not," said the flyer. "She wouldn't understand. I think we had better let the duck go."

"Don't let him go!" cried a voice. Norman came running up.

But it was too late. Flyer Frank already had let the young duck go and it flew quickly to its mother.

"Aw, shucks," said Norman.

He made up his mind to get a duck somehow. All during the time he and Honey Bunch and Flyer Frank walked around the Island to see the damage the storm had done, Norman kept trying to figure out a way to capture a baby duck.

"And when I do," he told himself, "I'm going to keep it for good. I'm going to take it home."

Now the little boy knew he was not supposed to go off by himself, but directly after breakfast he went to seek a baby duck. He crawled down the rocks to the place where the ducks were resting on the water.

Norman had one pocket full of corn. In the other he had a long piece of string. When he reached the water, the lad put a hole through one piece of corn and tied the string to it.

Holding the other end in his hand, he let the corn into the water as a fisherman would a piece of bait. He sat very still waiting for one of the ducks to come and grab it.

"Norman, Norman, where are you?" cried a voice from up above the little boy.

A duck was swimming toward the piece of bait. Norman kept very quiet.

"Norman, where are you?" It was Honey Bunch calling her playmate whom she had suddenly missed.

Norman wished she would keep still. The duck was almost at the piece of corn. When the bird snatched it with his bill, he would draw him in and grab the duck in his hands.

"Oh, there you are!" cried Honey Bunch. "What are you doing?"

At this very moment Norman's duck grabbed the piece of corn. The little boy leaned out over the water and yanked the line. So did the duck.

There was a brief struggle between the boy and the duck. Then plop! Norman went headfirst into the water!

CHAPTER VIII

OUT TO SEA

"OH, SOMEBODY come here quick!" cried Honey Bunch. "Norman's fallen in the water!"

The little girl screamed so loudly that all the Sampson family heard her and came running outside. Mr. Sampson, seeing the little girl pointing, scrambled down the rocks before he even knew what the trouble was. When he saw Norman struggling in the water, he leaped down even faster.

"Hold on, son!" he shouted.

Norman was too frightened to hold on to anything, though he might have caught hold of a near-by rock. Mr. Sampson jumped into the water and reached the boy a moment later.

It was not deep where Norman had fallen in, but it was over the little boy's head. Mr. Sampson waded out of the water and carried him to the level top of the Island.

"Norman! Norman!" Honey Bunch cried out. "Are you all right?"

Norman did know how to swim, but his sudden tumble into the water had made him forget everything except to hold his breath. He sputtered and coughed because he had swallowed some water, and his nose and ears and eyes were full of it. But in a few seconds he was all right.

"Whatever were you trying to do down there?" asked Mrs. Sampson, taking the little boy on her lap.

Norman told her. He also said he would never go near the water alone again. Suddenly he looked up at Mr. Sampson and said:

"You're a lifesaving man just like the dog Lucky."

Mr. Sampson suggested that perhaps the children would like to come to the top of the lighthouse with him and help put the big, green curtains over the light. This made Norman forget about the trouble he had been in. Honey Bunch, too, was eager to go up the spiral stairs and watch.

The sun was just starting to peep from behind the gray clouds as Mr. Sampson unfolded the last big, green curtain and finished covering the light. Norman and Honey Bunch felt very important because he held each of them up in turn and let them put the last section into place.

"And now," said Lightkeeper Sampson, "we'll see what's going on outside. Today is paint day here."

"What's paint day?" Honey Bunch asked.

The lightkeeper explained that every time they had a bad storm on Shell Horse Island some of the paint came off the white lighthouse. So that ships at sea could see it very clearly, the lighthouse had to be painted very often with a fresh coat of white paint.

They went down the stairs and out of the building. The two other men who worked on the Island were already putting a tall ladder against the tower. In a few moments, one of them took a bucket of paint and a brush and climbed the ladder.

"Oh, is he going all the way to the top?" Honey Bunch asked. "It seems so far, far up!"

"All the way to the roof," Mr. Sampson replied.

After the man had gone up, the other workman set a shorter ladder against the lighthouse. It reached about halfway up. Then he, too, took a bucket of paint and a brush and started to climb.

"Now, Steve," said Lightkeeper Sampson, "suppose you get busy, too."

"I don't want to work today," said Steve. "It's Sunday."

His father looked at him sternly. "Ships ride the seas on Sunday," he said. "The wind blows on Sunday. It rains on Sunday. When it's necessary, we paint on Sunday."

Steve mumbled, but he took a bucket of paint and a brush and went around to the far side.

Norman went around to watch him. Suddenly there was a loud squeal from the little boy.

Honey Bunch raced to see what had happened. What a sight Norman was! Steve had flicked a brushful of white paint on her playmate's only suit.

When Mrs. Sampson saw Norman's suit, she told Steve he would have to clean the little boy's clothes and also do all his father's painting.

Since Mr. Sampson was not going to do any

90

of the painting now, he offered to show the visitors his collection of shells. He kept them in a closet in the living room.

When he opened the door, the children gasped. Every wall and every shelf was covered with shells of all sizes and shapes. The lightkeeper pointed out the most interesting shells in the collection. He held up a thin, curlicue specimen.

"What do you think this is?" he asked.

Honey Bunch and Norman giggled. They said together, "A worm."

"And that's its name," the man laughed. "It's a Worm Shell. He's a funny fellow. He lives upside down, with the pointed end of his house buried in the sand."

Next Mr. Sampson held up a shell only one and a half inches long. He said it was called a Duck's Foot.

"It looks more like a tiny ice-cream cone," said Norman.

"Oh, I have a better ice-cream cone than this," said Mr. Sampson.

He reached to the back of one of the shelves and picked up a perfect cone shell about six inches long. It was light tan in color and had brown speckles on it, like an ice-cream cone which had been too well baked.

91

Norman thought it would be fun to put ice cream inside it, but the lightkeeper said the little boy would probably hurt his tongue trying to lick out the ice cream. Also, he might bite the shell by mistake and get a piece in his mouth.

"Here's one you might like better, Norman. It's a Yellow Helmet."

He set the big shell on the little boy's head.

Honey Bunch laughed. "It looks like a fireman's hat," she said, "even if it isn't red."

Secretly, Norman wished he could take the helmet home. How he would like to show a fireman's-helmet shell to his little friends in Barham!

"How do you like this, Honey Bunch?" the shell collector asked her.

He held up one which he said was very rare.

"It's just like a teeny, tiny umbrella," said the little girl.

Norman thought it looked like an umbrella too, but said it was no good, 'cause it had no handle.

"I can see you're a practical little person, Norman." The lightkeeper laughed. "So I'll tell you about one of the most practical of all the little animals that live in shells."

He picked up a small shell. Norman peeked

inside and remarked that there was nothing in it.

"Not now," Mr. Sampson explained, "but many years ago a little animal lived there."

Norman handed the shell to Honey Bunch. She thought the center looked like a fairy's tent. It was pink and blue and green.

"Listen to its lovely music," the lightkeeper suggested.

Honey Bunch held the shell to her ear. She heard a sound that was like a little bell ringing far away.

"The little animal who lived in this shell was called a Trochus," Lightkeeper Sampson said. "He had just one foot. When he was at home, he held this foot tightly against the opening, and no sea animal could come in and gobble him up."

"He was smart," Norman said. "What did he have besides a foot?"

"Two little horns on his head," Mr. Sampson answered. "And around his neck is a pretty, frilly collar. It has all the colors of the rainbow in it. You children may find a Trochus sometime, but they're shy little animals."

"How many kinds of shells are there in the whole wide world?" Honey Bunch asked.

"Just about sixty thousand," the lightkeeper replied.

This number was too big for either Honey Bunch or Norman to figure out.

"I hope, one of these days," said Mr. Sampson, "to add a big Shell Horse to my collection."

"Why'd you let Steve sell the one he had?" Norman spoke up.

"What do you mean?" Steve's father asked.

Now, Norman had not meant to be a tattletale. But the secret was out now.

Steve was called in. He hung his head and admitted having found the Shell Horse one day on the shore of the Island.

"I—I wanted some money," he said. "So I kept the shell a secret. One morning I took it with me when we flew to school and buried it in the sand on Sunrise Beach. These kids found it right after, but I got the shell back from them. Then I sold it when school was out."

"You remember, of course," said Steve's father, "that I have been wanting a Shell Horse for my collection, and you promised if you ever found one, to bring it to me."

"I remember," Steve answered, looking at the floor.

"I'll talk to you about this again, later," said his father. "It seems to me that ever since Honey Bunch and Norman have come to visit us, there's been nothing but trouble from you. Now, suppose you turn over a new leaf and be a good sport for a change."

"What do you want me to do?" Steve asked.

"Suppose," the lightkeeper suggested, "you take the children to the spot where you found the Shell Horse, and see if you can find another."

Steve, thankful he did not have to continue the work he was doing as punishment, led the way to a part of the Island where Honey Bunch and Norman had not been before. It was some little distance from where the flying boat was moored.

It was rocky along the shore, but there was one little level place with a pool of water. The water would almost drain out of the pool, then a big wave would splash over the rocks and fill it again.

"I found the Shell Horse right in this pool," said Steve.

The children took off their shoes and waded into the water.

"Somebody had better keep watch of the waves," said Steve, "or we'll get drenched."

"I'll watch," Priscilla offered.

She perched herself on a high rock and looked out over the ocean. The other children started digging in the sand of the pool. Honey Bunch had just struck something hard in the sand when Priscilla cried:

"Look out! Here comes a big wave!"

Honey Bunch, Norman and Steve hustled out of the little pool to higher rocks. A moment later, a big wave rolled in and filled the pool with water. As Norman started to wade into the pool again, Steve shouted a warning.

"It will be over your head. Wait a minute!"

At first Norman did not listen. But suddenly he remembered his tumble into the ocean before and thought he had better mind. He did not have long to wait. The water ran out between the cracks of the rocks very quickly, and the children jumped back in.

This time there was a long wait before Priscilla shouted again. In the meantime, the three other children had dug up several amusing but worthless objects. What Honey Bunch had felt before with her foot, and hoped was going to be a Shell Horse, turned out to be nothing but an old piece of iron. Norman found part of a frying pan. Steve came up with several clamshells.

Honey Bunch offered to change places with Priscilla, so the little Island girl let her be the lookout. Honey Bunch thought it was fun to watch the waves roll in and break.

These must be the sea combs, she thought. One time, when Mrs. Miller had told her a story about the seashore, she had said something about breaking waves being called sea combs. She decided to ask Steve about them.

"Steve!" Honey Bunch shouted above the roar of the water. "Are these sea combs?"

The big boy came running over. He thought Honey Bunch had found a piece of coral nicknamed a sea comb. When she pointed to the long, curling waves, he said in disgust:

"That's a comber, not a comb," and went back.

A few minutes later, Honey Bunch shouted again, and this time all the children hurried to where she stood.

"A boat's coming! A rowboat's coming in," she cried out.

Drifting toward Shell Horse Island was a boat which Steve said must have broken loose from some ocean-going tug.

"Let's get it!" he exclaimed.

The children ran along the shore. At some distance down, where the waves did not break so savagely, the boat came in. Steve scrambled into it.

"Bet I can sell this boat," he said.

"Daddy won't let you," his sister warned.

Steve ignored her. There was a long rope tied to the prow of the boat. The boy wound this around one of the rocks.

"I'll sell it if I want to," Steve declared.

"Let's hunt for Shell Horses here," suggested Priscilla, hoping to get her brother out of the boat.

Honey Bunch and Norman would rather have

played in the boat, but Priscilla thought they should not do this.

"It's all right. The boat's tied," said Steve.

"It's not all right," Priscilla argued. "If the rope should break, the boat would go out in the ocean again."

Norman thought it would be safe to take a chance and climbed up inside.

"I'm captain!" he shouted. "Steve, clean this boat up!"

Steve looked annoyed. "This is my boat," he said. "I'm the captain. You get out or I'll throw you in the water."

Norman did not want to get out, but he did not want to be thrown into the water either. He was inclined to think Steve meant what he said. The big boy had been nice enough for the past half-hour, but Norman was afraid this might not last. So he jumped out.

"I'm getting hungry," said Priscilla. "It must be dinnertime."

She started up the rocks. Norman followed. As Honey Bunch walked after them, Steve called to her.

"Hey, come back here," he said. "I want to try something."

Honey Bunch turned back. Steve was just climbing out of the boat.

"Do me a favor," he said. "Get in the boat and stand up in the middle."

"Why?" the little girl asked.

Steve explained that he thought it would make a good picture. The rocks, the boat and the little girl together looked like a famous painting he had once seen. He had a camera at the lighthouse. He would take a picture and maybe he could sell it.

"Wait here 'til I get my camera," he ordered.

Now, Honey Bunch had no intention of staying alone in the boat while Steve and the others went off. But, before she had a chance to climb out, a big wave came in. It yanked the rope loose from the rock.

Suddenly the boat was whirled around. The next thing Honey Bunch knew, it was several feet from shore.

"Steve! Steve!" she cried.

The big boy, who had started toward the lighthouse, turned around. He looked in terror at the sight before his eyes.

Honey Bunch Morton was being carried out to sea!

CHAPTER IX

A GREAT SURPRISE

THE waves carried Honey Bunch out farther and farther. Steve Sampson was scared.

"Can you swim, Honey Bunch?" he cried out.

"Only a little," Honey Bunch answered. She knew what the big boy was going to suggest. "I can't swim very far," she added, trying not to cry.

Steve looked around wildly. Nobody was in sight. He dived into the water and swam toward the drifting rowboat.

But the boat seemed to go faster than he could swim, and Steve grew more frightened every minute. He was a long way from shore now.

"I'll go back and get the motorboat," he shouted to Honey Bunch.

Steve just about managed to get back to the Island. He was so tired and out of breath from swimming that he could hardly stand up.

"Help! Help!" he tried to shout. But his voice was not very strong.

The boy pulled himself into the motorboat tied at the dock and tried to start the engine, but it would not turn over.

Steve was in a panic. He could hardly see Honey Bunch away out on the water now. The boat looked very small and Honey Bunch was a mere speck.

By this time the little girl was crying. She was trying to be brave, but it was very hard. She knew the best thing to do was to sit very still. Surely someone would come out and rescue her.

"Help! Help!" Steve shouted again.

His voice was stronger now. This time it was heard.

Flyer Frank came running down the slope to the Beach. Steve pointed out on the ocean.

"It's Honey Bunch!" he said.

Flyer Frank did not wait to hear any more. He tried to get the motorboat started, but he could not make it work, either.

Without waiting any longer, he ran into the water, swam out to his big flying boat, freed it from its moorings and climbed in. A second later he had its one good engine going.

The flying boat went skimming across the water. In a very short time Flyer Frank shut off the motor and drifted alongside Honey Bunch. He leaned out and said:

"Honey Bunch Morton, what were you trying to do? Cross the ocean all by yourself?"

The young man smiled as he left the window and made his way to the big side door in the plane. He opened the door and leaned far down, waiting for the rowboat to drift against the side, under the door. Then he told Honey Bunch to stand up slowly and stretch her arms above her head.

Quickly he grasped her wrists and pulled her up into the flying boat beside him. How glad she was!

Flyer Frank started his motor and headed back toward the Island. Honey Bunch wished they might bring the boat along, but the rope

had disappeared, and there was no way of towing the boat to the Island.

On the way back Flyer Frank asked the little girl what had happened. She did not like to tell him Steve had told her to get into the boat, but the pilot guessed it, anyway.

When they reached the Island, everyone was on the dock. Having heard the motor of the flying boat start up, they had come running to see what had happened. It was not until Honey Bunch looked out the window that they knew she had been rescued by Flyer Frank.

In the meantime, the two men who helped Mr. Sampson had fixed the motorboat, and one of them came out and took Honey Bunch and Flyer Frank off the plane.

Honey Bunch would not say a word against Steve, but the boy told the story himself. He said he had not meant to put Honey Bunch in danger, but his father declared Steve should have known better than to let her get into the boat. He took his son off to the lighthouse.

"Have you had enough boating for today?" Mrs. Sampson asked Honey Bunch. "Or would you like to go see the buoys?"

"Boys?" Honey Bunch asked, not understanding.

Mrs. Sampson explained that, to protect ships, a little floating tower is anchored in the water near big rocks or very shallow water. Inside the tower a bell rings all the time.

"What makes it work?" asked Norman, who was standing alongside Honey Bunch. He had decided to stay by her every minute, so nothing could happen to her again.

"The waves make the little tower rock, and then the bell rings," Mrs. Sampson answered.

"Doesn't it ever wear out?" Honey Bunch asked.

Steve's mother said that when it did, then someone had to go out and put a new bell in.

"But there's one bell not far from here that's been ringing for fifty years," she added.

Honey Bunch knew that this was a very long time. She just could not think of one bell ringing all the time for fifty years.

"Another kind of buoy whistles," said Mrs. Sampson.

"I haven't had too much boating," said Honey Bunch. "I'd like to see the bell buoys and the whistle buoys."

Mrs. Sampson said they would go out as soon as they had eaten dinner. By the time they finished, the ocean was very calm. Mrs. Sampson said they could not have picked a better time to go for the ride in the motorboat.

It was rather a long ride to the place where the first buoy was. Even when they were a long distance from it they could hear the bell going BING—BONG—BING—BONG. Mr. Sampson, who was steering the motorboat, made a big circle around the buoy. He told Honey Bunch and Norman and Priscilla, who had gone along, as well as Mrs. Sampson, to listen very hard to the bell.

"I'll hold my watch," he said, "and when a minute is up, I will tell you. See how many times the bell rings."

Honey Bunch thought this was a nice game. When Lightkeeper Sampson said, "Begin!" she started counting. When he said, "Stop," she had counted thirty.

"How many did you get, Norman?" the lightkeeper asked.

"Twenty-five," the little boy answered.

"Priscilla, how many did you count?" her father asked her.

"Twenty-eight."

"How about you, Honey Bunch?"

When she told him thirty, he said, "My, my,

you little folks didn't get together very well. Suppose you count again."

The next time Honey Bunch got thirty again. Norman and Priscilla each got twenty-nine.

"Did you count, Mom?" the lightkeeper asked his wife.

Mrs. Sampson smiled and said, "I guess we'll have to give Honey Bunch Morton the prize. It rang thirty both times."

"I'll bet Norman will win the next game," said Lightkeeper Sampson, smiling, as he steered the motorboat in another direction.

In the distance they could see an island. Mrs. Sampson said this was Pine Tree Island, one of the places where people lived only in the summertime. No one was there yet.

"What's the game I can win?" Norman asked eagerly.

"The whistling-buoy game," Mr. Sampson answered.

A few minutes later the children could hear a sound like wind. It reminded Honey Bunch of the noise the great wind had made.

Presently they saw the whistling buoy. It looked very much like the bell buoy.

"In this game I want you to be last, Norman,"

107

said Mr. Sampson. "Honey Bunch, you start. See if you can make a sound like the whistling buoy."

Honey Bunch tried very hard, but it was a weak little wind. Priscilla tried next. She could not do any better than Honey Bunch.

"All right, Norman, go ahead," Lightkeeper Sampson said laughingly, "and don't fail me."

Norman sucked in his breath very hard until he was red in the face, then he let it out slowly between his teeth. It made a tremendous whistling sound.

"What do you think, Mom?"

"It's too cheerful," Priscilla's mother replied. "Try to make it kind of mournful."

Norman tried several times. Finally he got it perfect. He even made the game better. First the buoy in the water would whistle, then the little boy in the boat would whistle.

Norman liked the game so much he did not want to go home. But Mr. Sampson said they had better return to Shell Horse Island.

"You have to be careful when you're out on the ocean," he said. "The water doesn't stay calm very long."

He put on full speed and the motorboat skipped across the water with a kind of *spank-spank* sound. It was about four o'clock when they reached Shell Horse Island. Mr. Sampson suggested that if Honey Bunch and Norman were not tired, he would show them the old shipwreck.

"On this island?" the little girl asked him.

"Yes," the lightkeeper answered. "It happened a long, long time ago, before the lighthouse was built here."

He took the children down an iron ladder, just below the big tower. At this point the rocks were too dangerous and slippery for anyone to climb up and down them without a ladder.

"Hold on very tight," he warned the children.

They did. Even Norman did not try to figure out any better way to get down. When they reached the foot of the ladder, Mr. Sampson, who had gone first, held Honey Bunch and Norman by the hand.

"Now walk very carefully," he directed.

The three of them climbed across some rocks. In a moment they saw the prow of an old ship. Mr. Sampson said it was all that was left of what had once been a proud sailing vessel.

"Can we go inside the old boat?" Norman asked.

"Well, I guess so," the lightkeeper answered,

looking out over the water. "The tide won't be in for a bit."

When they stepped among the rocks and sand in which the old ship was half buried, Norman was delighted. He put one hand over his eyes like a sunshade, struck a pose and looked out over the water.

"I'm the captain of the pea-green boat," he said. This was the oldest boat he could remember having heard about.

Honey Bunch giggled. "Are you an owl or a pussy cat?" she asked.

Mr. Sampson smiled. "Quite a boat, Norman," he said. "What kind of cargo do you carry?"

"I carry whales."

"Then I guess that's how you got shipwrecked," said Honey Bunch. "Whales are awful heavy."

For a moment Norman had forgotten he was standing on a wreck. He could not think of any more exciting way to be shipwrecked than by a whale, so he said he guessed Honey Bunch was right.

"We'd better go back to the lighthouse now," said Mr. Sampson. "And remember, Norman, you are no longer a captain, and you must not come down to the wreck by yourself. The tide might be coming in and then you would be in trouble."

The little boy promised. The lightkeeper said his orders applied to Honey Bunch as well, and she, too, promised not to go down there alone.

Flyer Frank was waiting for them when they reached the top of the cliff. He thought the children had had such a long, exciting day that they should go to bed soon after supper.

"I'm expecting the new part for my flying boat early in the morning," he said. "As soon as the motor is fixed, we'll take off."

But when morning came, neither a plane nor a boat arrived at Shell Horse Island with the part for the engine. Flyer Frank was annoyed.

"No school for you and Priscilla today," he said to Steve at the breakfast table. "I can't risk it on one motor."

"Can't hurt my feelings," Steve replied. "I don't like school, anyway."

"Maybe," his mother remarked, "if you'd pay more attention to your studies, you'd like school better."

Steve said no more about school. When he started out of the house, Honey Bunch ran after him.

"Steve," she said, "if you don't have to work, let's go hunt for Shell Horses again."

"All right," said Steve. "But there's no use going to the pool where I found the other one."

By this time Norman and Priscilla had come out of the Sampson house and were eager to go along too.

Steve said he knew another place where there was a little sandy pool. They could try that. It was on the side of the island facing the mainland. When they climbed down, Honey Bunch exclaimed:

"Oh, it's a fishpool!"

Sure enough, in the pool, which had about a foot of water in it, several small fish were swimming around.

"Whoops!" Steve exclaimed. "They're good eating."

"Let's catch some," said Priscilla.

Honey Bunch and Norman wondered how this could be done. The Sampson children had no fish poles, lines, or nets.

The brother and sister took off their shoes and waded into the pool. They held their shoes in the water, and as a fish swam toward them they would capture it in the toe of a shoe.

When he and Priscilla had caught all the fish, Steve took them back to the lighthouse, saying he would return in a minute.

Honey Bunch and Norman took off their shoes and stepped into the water to look for Shell Horses.

"I've got something!" Norman cried out.

The little boy dug in the sand and finally pulled up something.

"Aw, shucks," he said. "It's just a clam!"

"I never saw such a big one!" Priscilla said.

Norman felt better. Maybe he had found the

biggest clam anybody had ever dug up. He decided to run back to the lighthouse and show it to Mr. Sampson.

When Norman reached the tower, he met Steve just starting back. Norman showed him the clam.

"It's sure big," he said, "and there might be a pearl inside. It's mostly oysters that have pearls inside, but once in a while a clam does."

He opened the clam with his penknife. There was a tiny pearl inside.

"It's not worth much," said Steve, but Norman was happy about the pearl just the same.

In the meantime, Honey Bunch and Priscilla were still looking for a Shell Horse. Several times the little girls had thought they were about to get one, only to dig up a shell of another variety.

Suddenly Honey Bunch's fingers felt something sharp down in the sand of the pool. She pulled and pulled but could not get the object up.

"Priscilla, help me," she cried excitedly.

Priscilla waded over. Together the two little girls got hold of the sharp point and gave a tremendous yank. Both of them sat down hard in the water. But in Honey Bunch's hands was a large shell. Did she dare believe her own eyes?

"Is it a Shell Horse?" she asked Priscilla excitedly.

"Oh, I'm sure it is!" exclaimed the little Island girl.

Honey Bunch and Priscilla quickly put on their shoes, climbed the rocks and started toward the lighthouse. Honey Bunch hugged her precious find.

Priscilla shouted to Steve and Norman who were walking toward them. Suddenly Honey Bunch had a feeling Steve would take the Shell Horse away from her, so she walked over close to the edge of the cliff, trying to hide the big shell.

But Steve knew something was up. He came running over.

"You found a Shell Horse!" he cried. "Let me have it!"

"No!" Honey Bunch cried out.

Steve tried to take the shell away from her. In swinging her arm back to avoid him, the little girl's fingers lost their grip.

A moment later the precious Shell Horse went bounding down the cliff!

CHAPTER X

HONEY BUNCH IS WORRIED

"STEVE, you bad, bad boy!" Priscilla screamed, stamping her foot in anger.

Honey Bunch held back the tears that wanted to run down her cheeks. All of the children had worked so hard to find a Shell Horse. She had uncovered a really fine one, and now it was gone.

Steve Sampson had started to climb down the rocks after it. Priscilla went after him and grabbed his arm.

"It's Honey Bunch's Shell Horse!" she cried out. "You can't have it!"

Steve kept on. This time Norman climbed down and held onto him, too.

"Honey Bunch, you go get it," said Priscilla. "We'll hold Steve."

"Aw, it's probably all busted, anyway," the big boy said. "If Honey Bunch wants it bad enough to climb down and get it, she can have it."

Steve went back to the lighthouse. Honey Bunch climbed down the rocks to where she could see the Shell Horse just showing around the corner of a rock. She went very carefully, because the rocks were sharp. It took her a good many minutes.

Priscilla and Norman waited for her at the top. Norman began to grow impatient. He was sure he could have gone down in half the time.

"Girls are poky old things," he said to Priscilla.

"They are not!" Priscilla defended herself and all other little girls. "They're just careful. They don't do crazy things like boys. They don't fall in the water and let people drift off alone in boats."

Norman said no more. There might be something to what Priscilla was saying. He remembered that Mrs. Miller had said he was a two-and-two child, which he felt sure was something not very good. He hoped to find out some day what a two-and-two child really was.

By this time Honey Bunch had reached the water's edge where the Shell Horse lay. She picked it up.

"It's not hurt much," she called up to her friends. "I think it will be all right for your daddy, Priscilla."

Honey Bunch started the steep climb back up

117

with her precious shell. But suddenly the little girl found she could not make any progress. She would go three feet and slip back two, because the rocks were wet from the spray.

"Oh, dear, what am I going to do?" she thought.

Honey Bunch tried getting up the embankment once more. It was no use.

"Say, what's the matter with you?" Norman called down. "You're an old slowpoke."

"I can't get up," Honey Bunch answered.

Priscilla had lived on the Island since she was a baby, so the little girl knew exactly why Honey Bunch was having such trouble. She also knew just what to do.

"Walk along the shore," she suggested. "Norman and I will walk along up here. There's a

place where you can climb up easily. I'll show you."

Honey Bunch was glad to hear this. She did what Priscilla told her. But there was no path, and it was hard to keep from stumbling. Honey Bunch had to jump from rock to rock. Some of them were pointed and off she went.

After she had walked about five minutes, Honey Bunch came to a place where the ocean ran right under the rocky cliff.

"It's just like a cave," she thought.

The little girl stood still and looked. Something was lying on top of the water, wedged in tightly between two rocks. Honey Bunch wondered what it was. It looked like part of a boat, but it was not a boat. It was yellow in color.

For a few minutes Honey Bunch had been out of sight of the children above her. When she did not appear, they became frightened and started calling.

"Honey Bunch, where are you?"

"I'm all right. There's something funny down here."

Norman was very curious to know what it was. He thought of climbing down, but Priscilla stopped him.

"This is a bad place on the Island," she said. "Lots of shipwrecks come in here."

"Is that what Honey Bunch is looking at?" Norman asked.

"Prob'ly," Priscilla answered.

Honey Bunch already had decided that this big yellow thing in the water probably was part of a shipwreck. She looked around to see if there were any other parts of a ship, but she could not see anything. Finally, she left the spot and went on. In another five minutes Priscilla called down to her.

"This is the place to come up, Honey Bunch. See that little path between the rocks?"

Honey Bunch could see the path very plainly. It went zigzagging up the embankment to the top. Soon she was safely alongside her friends.

Priscilla wanted to see the condition of the Shell Horse. Norman was more interested in hearing what Honey Bunch had seen down by the cave. He was disappointed when he heard it was not a whole ship.

"I thought we could go play in it," he said. "One old piece isn't any good."

The three children hurried to the lighthouse. Honey Bunch ran to find Mr. Sampson and proudly handed him the big shell she had found.

"Well, I never!" exclaimed the collector, as he thanked Honey Bunch. "To think that a little girl who doesn't even live near the seashore would be the one to give me this. And to have found it practically on my own doorstep, too! I wonder where the Shell Horse lived when he was alive."

"Mrs. Miller says, 'Chickens come home to roost,'" Honey Bunch quoted. "Maybe this Shell Horse was born here, and went on a trip, and came back."

"How could he get anywhere else?" Norman asked.

"By crawling along the ocean bottom," Mr. Sampson answered. "He might have gone over to Pine Tree Island for instance. That's the one I showed you yesterday where the people stay only in the summertime."

The children went into the Sampson kitchen where Mrs. Sampson was baking cookies. She had the radio turned on. As Honey Bunch stepped into the kitchen, she heard the announcer say:

"A news item has just come in about the famous Dr. Hopewell and his equally famous dog Lucky. The doctor started off Saturday evening on a flight with some rare medicine for a sick child up North. No word has been heard from him since."

The radio announcer went on to other news. Honey Bunch did not hear him. She rushed up to Mrs. Sampson and said, with tears in her eyes:

"Oh, Mrs. Sampson, you don't s'pose Dr. Hopewell and Lucky had to come down, the same as we did? And—and—maybe this time Lucky wasn't lucky?"

Mrs. Sampson put her arm around the little girl. She said there was no reason to believe the doctor and his dog were not all right. Flyers often had trouble with their planes and had to come down in out-of-the-way places. Sometimes they had to walk a long distance to get to a farmhouse or to a town.

Honey Bunch was comforted for a little while.

Then she started to worry all over again. Maybe Dr. Hopewell and Lucky had been caught in the big storm. She asked Mrs. Sampson to turn on the radio again. Presently there was another report about the doctor.

"Flyers are out searching for Dr. Hopewell and Lucky," the announcer said. "It is thought that he may have been forced down in Saturday night's bad storm. It is not known what route he took. Friends of the doctor are hopeful that since he did not radio for help from his plane, he may be all right."

"But maybe his radio didn't work," spoke up Norman, who was standing close to Honey Bunch. "Sometimes in a bad storm our radio at home doesn't work."

Honey Bunch was dreadfully upset. She went off by herself and thought very hard. Mother had often told her that it might help a person in trouble if his friends thought good thoughts about him very hard. So Honey Bunch kept saying over and over to herself:

"Of course Dr. Hopewell's all right. Of course Lucky is all right. We're going to hear from them pretty soon."

Norman came to ask her what she was doing.

She told him. Norman thought this might help, but he wished there was something practical he could be doing.

"Like what?" Honey Bunch asked him.

"Like going out in a boat to rescue him," the little boy replied. "Maybe Dr. Hopewell and Lucky came down on the water."

Honey Bunch gave a little cry of dismay. This would be dreadful! Dr. Hopewell's plane was not a flying boat. If it should come down on the water, it surely would sink!

Honey Bunch jumped up from the chair on which she was sitting and ran off to find Mr. Sampson. He was high up in the tower of the lighthouse, polishing the light so that its beams could be seen better far out over the ocean.

"Mr. Sampson," said Honey Bunch, "do you think Dr. Hopewell's airplane fell in the water?"

"I don't know," he replied. "I'm not sure whether he was flying over the ocean or not."

"Please, will you find out?" Honey Bunch begged.

Mr. Sampson looked into Honey Bunch's clear, blue eyes. "I'll do my best," he told her. "Come with me."

Together they climbed up to the top landing

of the lighthouse. Mr. Sampson picked up a radio telephone and talked to a man on the shore.

"The Coast Guard says the doctor's ship might have been blown out over the ocean right near here," he said. "Let's look at this map."

Mr. Sampson led Honey Bunch over to a big map on the wall. He took a little black pin and pressed it into the map.

"Here is where Dr. Hopewell started," he said. Then his finger traced a long line to the north. He put another pin in the map. "And this is the spot he was heading for."

"Would he go in a straight line?" Honey Bunch asked.

"Probably not, if the weather was bad," the lightkeeper said. "If he went this side of the mountains, he would be nearer the ocean, and it's the shorter route."

"And he was in a hurry to start off on Saturday," said Honey Bunch. "The sick little girl needed the medicine very much. Mr. Sampson, do you s'pose Dr. Hopewell and Lucky flew right over Shell Horse Island that night?"

A look of excitement came into Mr. Sampson's eyes. "If Dr. Hopewell did take the shorter route, and if he was blown off his course that night," he said, "he might have flown right over Shell Horse Island!"

Tears came into Honey Bunch's eyes. "Then the doctor and Lucky could have fallen into the ocean right near here!" She began to sob. "Mr. Sampson, will you come to a cave with me? I— saw something there—and it might be—oh, I hope not!"

"What is it, dear?" the man asked kindly.

Honey Bunch told him about the yellow thing she had seen wedged in the rocks. When Mr. Sampson heard about it, he said, "Come, Honey Bunch! We'll go look at it right away."

Together they hurried down the stairs of the lighthouse. Norman saw them and tagged along.

"Where are you going?" he asked.

"To look at that yellow thing," Honey Bunch answered. "It—it might be part of the plane Lucky was on!"

CHAPTER XI

THE SEARCH

NORMAN became so excited that he ran around shouting:

"Hurry up, everybody! Come and see what Honey Bunch has found!"

Of course Norman did not really know himself what it was that Honey Bunch had found. But Mrs. Sampson and Steve and the other families on the Island hurried outside excitedly. The men followed the lightkeeper and the little girl.

Honey Bunch hoped with all her heart that the thing she had seen wedged between the rocks was not part of Dr. Hopewell's plane. But something inside her kept telling the little girl it was. Soon they were on the cliff above the cave.

"I can't climb down the steep rocks very well, Mr. Sampson," Honey Bunch said, "but I can go down the path all by myself."

"Then we'll go that way," he said.

Lightkeeper Sampson knew the path very well. He had gone down it many times because of shipwrecks, but thanks to his light, there had been none for a long time.

When they reached the beach, Honey Bunch pointed out the yellow object she had seen.

"It's part of an airplane wing all right," said Mr. Sampson. Then, turning the wing over, he saw some numbers on it.

"Did either of the wings of Dr. Hopewell's plane have 41-H painted on it?" he asked Honey Bunch.

When the little girl said she could not remember, the lightkeeper said he would find out right away.

He and the others went back up the rocky path. The lightkeeper at once radioed the Coast Guard. He asked them to find out the full number of Dr. Hopewell's plane. It seemed to

Honey Bunch as if the answer would never come. The children went outside and tried to play. But nothing seemed to be much fun.

"I wish they'd hurry," Honey Bunch said over and over.

Finally she saw Mr. Sampson coming out of the lighthouse.

"Mr. Sampson," she cried, running to meet him, "have you heard yet?"

The lightkeeper did not answer her at once. He picked Honey Bunch up in his arms and looked at her very soberly.

"I'm afraid," he said, "that your guess may be right. Dr. Hopewell's plane had a long number and part of it was 41-H. The people who have charge of the registration of planes are looking up all the flyers whose plane numbers have 41-H in them."

"Then they haven't found Dr. Hopewell and Lucky?" she asked.

"Not yet. Flyers are still out looking for him. As soon as all planes with 41-H on them are checked, they're going to start a search out this way."

Mr. Sampson explained that the Coast Guard would send out their motor launches, too, to cover every part of the water.

"Do you think they can find the doctor and his dog?" Honey Bunch asked. "Could—could they still be floating on the water?" The little girl was trying very hard not to cry.

"It's very possible Dr. Hopewell and Lucky are floating around on a piece of the wreckage of his plane, if they were forced down on the ocean. But please stop worrying, Honey Bunch," the lightkeeper begged. "They may be all right and perfectly safe somewhere else, you know. Just because no one has heard from them doesn't mean they aren't all right."

Honey Bunch was not convinced. She knew Dr. Hopewell had been anxious to get the rare medicine to the sick child up North. The doctor would certainly try to get somebody to fly him, if his own plane had gone down.

A few minutes later, Mr. Sampson heard over the radio that every plane whose number contained 41-H was accounted for except Dr. Hopewell's. He must have been blown off his course during the hurricane, but where he had come down was a mystery. When Honey Bunch was told this, she said:

"If one of his wings is here, he must have come down here!"

Lightkeeper Sampson explained that in such

a bad storm, bits of wreckage were carried miles and miles away from where a ship or a plane might have had trouble.

"The doctor may be far, far away from here. The waves could have carried part of the wing to this island and wedged it in among the rocks."

Honey Bunch thought about this for a few minutes, then she said, "Maybe he came down near here, and he was carried out to sea as I was in the rowboat."

"Yes, that could have happened," said Mr. Sampson. "How would you like to look through my big spyglass and watch for the Coast Guard launches and the planes that are going to search for the doctor?"

"And Lucky," said Honey Bunch.

The men *must* find the doctor and his wonderful dog, Honey Bunch thought. Both of them had saved so many lives. Now somebody must save them if they were drifting on the ocean.

Mr. Sampson went into the house and took his long spyglass from a leather case. Then he and Honey Bunch and Norman went up the winding stairs of the lighthouse. Norman had become very quiet. He was very fond of Lucky.

They went to the second landing. The light-keeper opened the heavy window.

131

"We'll look from here first," he said.

He held the spyglass to one eye and gazed out over the water. He could not see anything, so he said it probably was too early yet for the planes and the launches to have reached Shell Horse Island.

"Tell us about a shipwreck," said Norman, as they sat down to wait.

"All right," said Mr. Sampson. "Would you like to hear about the big sailing ship that got lost?"

"Oh, yes," said Norman. Norman loved sailboats. "Was it a racing sailboat?" he asked.

"That's right, little man," said Mr. Sampson. "There was a big race across the ocean one time," he said. "One of the boats got off its course when a big storm came up. In the darkness the captain did not know where he was."

"What did he do?" Norman asked.

"There was not much he could do until finally he saw our big light here, beaming out over the dark ocean. He knew our signal, and what do you think happened?"

"Did he get shipwrecked here?"

"Oh, no," said Lightkeeper Sampson. "When he saw our light and knew where he was, the

132

captain turned his boat around and got back on the course."

"Was he the last one in?" said Norman.

Mr. Sampson smiled. "That's the funny part of the story," he said. "He was the first one in, and won the prize. In the storm, all the other captains got off the course, too, but they didn't see the big light on Shell Horse Island, so they all came in late."

Honey Bunch smiled. "Did you get a prize, too," she asked Mr. Sampson, "for lending the captain your fingers?"

The man was puzzled by what she meant. Then he smiled.

"I guess you mean 'lending a hand,'" he said. He already had heard the little girl use several quaint expressions she had picked up from the Mortons' laundress. "Yes, I did get a little prize," he answered. "The captain sent me, of all things, a cow! But it was a mighty good gift."

Honey Bunch thought she heard a plane overhead, so she jumped up and went to the window. Mr. Sampson showed her how to hold the long glass to her eye. In a moment she saw a big plane through the spyglass.

"They're here!" she cried out. "Now they're

133

surely going to find Dr. Hopewell and Lucky."

Soon she saw another plane and then another. A little while later she saw a big motor launch approaching on the water.

Then Norman took the big, long glass. What he saw made the little boy so excited that he almost dropped the spyglass. A helicopter was coming toward them!

"It goes like an eggbeater," Norman remarked, giggling. "It looks like a banana."

Indeed, the helicopter did look like a big black banana with the whirring blades of an eggbeater on top. It could remain still in the air.

"What's he going to do?" Norman cried.

"If they find Dr. Hopewell," said Mr. Sampson, "they'll let down a rope and pull him right up inside the helicopter."

The planes and the boats had come very suddenly. It seemed no time at all before they all went away.

"Where are they going now?" Honey Bunch asked Mr. Sampson.

"Farther out to sea, I guess."

Honey Bunch looked through the spyglass as long as she could see any of the planes or the boats.

"I guess we'll have to follow the rest of the search over the radio," said the lightkeeper. "Suppose we go into the house and listen."

He tuned the radio to various stations, but there was no news about Dr. Hopewell and Lucky.

Mrs. Sampson said, "No news is good news."

"I hope you're right," said Honey Bunch, sighing just as Mrs. Miller did when she was wishing very hard for something.

The children grew restless, and Mrs. Sampson suggested that they go outside and play.

"Tell you what," said Norman, "let's go down and see if Flyer Frank's plane is fixed. I'll bet one of those boats brought the new part for the engine. If he gets it fixed, maybe he'll take us up and we can hunt, too."

Honey Bunch thought this was a thrilling

idea. She and Priscilla ran along with Norman.

Flyer Frank was tinkering with his flying boat, but he said the new part had not come yet. It might not come until the next day.

Suddenly the little girl saw something moving in the water. It was coming toward the Island. Was it a big fish, or maybe a seal?

"No," she told herself. "It—it looks like—"

Honey Bunch ran down to the water's edge. She looked very hard. Now she knew. It was a dog swimming toward the Island.

It was the head of a collie.

In a few moments the dog dragged itself from the water and lay down, panting, on the beach. Honey Bunch leaned over it. Then she cried out joyfully:

"It's Lucky! Lucky is here!"

CHAPTER XII

NORMAN'S DISCOVERY

EVERYONE came running to Honey Bunch's side to see the famous dog. Lucky lay panting on the beach. Honey Bunch sat down and hugged him.

"Oh, Lucky, I'm so glad you're safe," she said. "You poor, poor dog! Where have you come from? You're so tired!"

Lucky was tired indeed. Flyer Frank said he must have swum a long distance.

"How far, do you think?" Honey Bunch asked him.

"It's hard to say," the pilot answered. "Dogs have been known to stay in the water for long periods."

Honey Bunch was sure Lucky's master *must* be at the place from which the dog had come. Flyer Frank said she might be right, but he doubted it.

"I'm more inclined to think," he said, "that the plane came down on the water and Dr.

Hopewell and Lucky were separated. But just the same this is a good clue."

When Honey Bunch asked what a clue was, Flyer Frank said it was like finding a missing piece to a jigsaw puzzle. Then he hurried to the radiotelephone to notify the Coast Guard that Honey Bunch had found Dr. Hopewell's dog on Shell Horse Island.

"When they locate the doctor," the flyer said to Honey Bunch, returning to the beach, "he will be glad to hear his pet is safe."

The children agreed. But time went on and no news came of Dr. Hopewell. Honey Bunch started worrying all over again. Flyer Frank told her that the Coast Guard was very efficient. If the doctor were anywhere in the area where part of his plane's wing had been found, they certainly would locate him.

"You know what?" said Norman. "I'll bet Lucky has been sitting out on one of those bell buoys."

"He couldn't stick on," said Priscilla. "They're too slippery."

"I'll bet he was floating on a piece of wreckage," suggested Steve, who had come down from the lighthouse when he heard the excitement.

Honey Bunch became very quiet. She sat

down on the ground beside Lucky and patted him. The dog laid his head on her lap and closed his eyes.

"You take a little nap," said Honey Bunch.

Lucky seemed to recognize Honey Bunch and not want to leave her.

Norman was a bit jealous. He felt that he knew Lucky as well as Honey Bunch did. But he knew dogs were very smart and remembered things a long time.

"Maybe he remembers how I let Honey Bunch's dog out of the car and he nearly got run over by Flyer Frank's plane," the little boy told himself.

Priscilla and Norman ran up to the lighthouse and came back with a plate of meat and vegetables and a pan of fresh water for Lucky.

"Here, Lucky," Norman said, setting the plate of food down near the dog.

Lucky did not stir. He raised his head, sniffed, and put his nose back in Honey Bunch's lap.

"I guess he's not hungry after all," said Priscilla.

"More than likely he's too tired to eat," suggested Flyer Frank. "Lucky looks pretty exhausted to me."

Honey Bunch thought about this for several seconds. Any dog should be hungry after a long swim, she decided. There must be some other reason why Lucky would not eat.

"Maybe he's sick," she thought.

She felt his nose, which she knew would be hot if he were not feeling well. Lucky's nose was quite cold. Suddenly an idea came to the little girl.

"I know why he won't eat!" she exclaimed. "He's been taught never to take food from strangers."

"You mean he'd starve before he'd take food from a stranger?" Norman asked.

"Honey Bunch is right," said Flyer Frank. "We're not exactly strangers to Lucky, but we have never given him food before, so he won't take it from us now. But maybe he'll drink some fresh water if Honey Bunch gives it to him."

Norman brought over the pan of water.

Honey Bunch gently urged the tired dog to drink, until finally he had lapped up all the water.

When Lucky was through, Norman said he wanted to show the dog the Island. Flyer Frank doubted that Lucky would be interested.

"I think Lucky would rather go up to the barn and have a good sleep."

The children had to coax and coax before Lucky would leave the beach. But finally, when Honey Bunch started off, he followed close at her heels. The children made a soft bed of hay in the barn and Lucky flopped down gratefully.

"We'd better go now," said Honey Bunch. "Let's run back to the house. Maybe there's some news about Lucky's master."

Mrs. Sampson had the radio on, but she told the children there had been no more special bulletins about the missing doctor.

"I'll let you know the minute I hear anything," she promised. "You may as well go out and play."

"I know what let's do," said Norman. "You promised to show me the cave, Honey Bunch. Maybe some more of Dr. Hopewell's plane is inside it."

"All right," said the little girl.

She led the way down the narrow, rocky path. The piece of the plane wing was still there.

The children decided that to get into the cave they would have to climb in over the rocks.

Norman went first, but it was hard work. He tore his clothes and his shoes were wet.

"You girls better not come," he said.

"Why not?" Priscilla answered. "I know these rocks better than you do."

Finally the three children reached the little cavelike opening in the Island.

"I see something!" Norman yelled. "Finders, keepers!"

Up among the rocks in the cave was a small black package. The children could not reach it, though they tried very hard and nearly tumbled into the water.

"Let's get Flyer Frank," Honey Bunch suggested. "He can reach it."

"Okay," said Norman, and went with the girls.

The pilot was still working on his plane. The new part had not yet come, and he was trying to fix up the old motor as best he could. He had borrowed some wires and pieces of metal and also a soldering iron.

"Hello, children," he said. "I'm trying to get this motor going somehow. We've got to get the Island children back to school."

Norman shouted that they had found something in the cave and needed his help to get it out.

"It might be something from Dr. Hopewell's plane," Honey Bunch told the young man.

Flyer Frank went with the children at once. It was hard even for him to reach the black package. But by sprawling flat on the rocks above the cave and stretching his arm away down inside, he could just get hold of it with his fingers.

"What is it?" Norman cried. "I found it. It's mine."

Flyer Frank smiled. "Maybe you won't want it, Norman. We don't even know what it is."

143

Crowding around him, the children saw that the package was wrapped in an oilskin.

Flyer Frank took the oilskin off. Inside was a white box marked:

DO NOT EXPOSE TO DAMPNESS.

"We'd better not open it," said the flyer. "We'll take it to the lighthouse for safekeeping."

Flyer Frank gave the package to Mrs. Sampson and asked her too keep it in a dry place.

The children decided to go and see how Lucky was. To their surprise the dog had left the barn. They whistled and called, but he did not answer.

"Maybe he swam away again," said Norman.

"Oh dear!" cried Honey Bunch.

She ran down to the beach where Lucky had come in. Then the little girl sighed in relief. There stood Lucky, looking out over the water.

"Are you thinking about your master?" the little girl asked him.

The beautiful dog looked up at her as if he were trying to tell her something.

"Do you know where your master is?"

Lucky's dark eyes lighted and he wagged his tail, barking sharply.

"Oh, dear," said Honey Bunch. "I wish I understood dog language."

Lucky went to the edge of the water, pawed at a little wave that rippled in and looked at Honey Bunch alertly.

"What is it, Lucky?"

The little girl walked close to the water's edge. She reached down and got her fingers wet. Lucky became excited and dashed into the shallow water, barking. Honey Bunch had an idea. She took off her shoes and waded in.

This time Lucky became really excited and barked even louder. Honey Bunch looked straight at him. Again she said:

"Do you know where your master is?"

Lucky began to swim out, but when he found the little girl was not following him, he came back. She looked at the dog very hard. Then suddenly she exclaimed:

"I know what you're trying to tell me!"

Without bothering to put her shoes back on, Honey Bunch ran to the edge of the dock and called to the pilot, who was tinkering with his plane.

"Flyer Frank! Flyer Frank!" she cried. "I've guessed Lucky's secret!"

The young man poked his head out of the window of his plane and asked her what she meant. Honey Bunch told him how strangely Lucky had acted during the past few minutes and then said:

"I'm sure Lucky knows where Dr. Hopewell is. If somebody will swim with him, Lucky will take him to his master."

Flyer Frank could not believe Honey Bunch was right, but he was willing to try the experiment.

"I have some bathing trunks in the plane," he told her. "I'll put them on and swim out a little way with the dog. Then we'll see if you're right."

The young man appeared in a couple of minutes dressed for the swim. Lucky seemed to know what was going to happen. He pranced around excitedly, barking thunderously.

"Well, here goes!" said Flyer Frank.

He ran into the water and dived into the surf.

146

Lucky followed him and started swimming very fast. Flyer Frank waited for him. In a few moments the dog passed him and set out for deeper water. Flyer Frank went after him.

"Oh, it worked! It worked!" Honey Bunch cried, jumping up and down.

Flyer Frank now knew the little girl was right, but he did not dare go off alone with the dog. He had no idea how far out Lucky might take him.

"Lucky, I'm going back," he shouted to the dog. "Lucky! Lucky!"

The dog turned his head. Flyer Frank started back for the beach. For a moment Honey Bunch was afraid the dog would not return. But presently he turned around.

"Honey Bunch, run up to the lighthouse and tell Mr. Sampson we'd like to take the motorboat out and follow Lucky," the flyer told her.

Honey Bunch had never run faster in her life. Norman and Priscilla, seeing her, wanted to know what had happened. She told them as she sped past.

All the people on the Island came down to the beach. Since everyone could not go in the motorboat, Mr. Sampson decided that only Flyer Frank, Steve, Norman and the two girls would go with him. They climbed into the boat and left the dock.

To their amazement, Lucky stood on the shore. They whistled and called to him, but he did not move.

Mr. Sampson turned to Honey Bunch. "You're a very good friend of Lucky's," he said. "What do you think we should do?"

"I think," said Honey Bunch, "that somebody has to swim with the dog."

Mr. Sampson slapped his knee. "I believe you're right," he said.

"Let me," offered Steve.

"I'll go," said Flyer Frank. "I'm the only one who has a swim suit on."

Mr. Sampson let him off at the dock, and once more he started out from shore with Lucky. This time he did not leave the dog's side.

"Gosh," said Norman, "look at Lucky go. He's a swell swimmer."

The motorboat slowly followed behind them. Honey Bunch was so excited that she was breathing very fast.

Was Lucky going to lead them somewhere over the water to Dr. Hopewell?

CHAPTER XIII

FOUND!

THE motorboat was running at low speed in order to stay behind Flyer Frank and Lucky. The dog was swimming strongly, but his speed was slow compared to that of a motorboat.

Honey Bunch stood in the prow, looking from left to right for any sign of an airplane or a piece of wreckage. It did not seem possible that the launch and the planes of the Coast Guard could have missed anything, but Lucky seemed to know exactly where he was headed.

"This way is toward the mainland, isn't it?" Honey Bunch asked Mr. Sampson.

"That's right," the lightkeeper answered.

"Where do you s'pose Lucky's going to take us?" the little girl questioned him.

"I haven't the least idea," Priscilla's father replied, "and I don't want you to be disappointed if we don't find Dr. Hopewell. Lucky may have some other reason for wanting us to follow him."

149

After Flyer Frank had gone about half a mile at a good clip, he dropped behind the dog and swam over to the boat.

"I'm getting a bit tired," he said. "I think I'll climb in."

Steve helped hoist him aboard and put a coat around the flyer's shoulders. Lucky looked back. Seeing that his companion had deserted him, he came to the boat.

"Now what's up?" said Mr. Sampson.

He turned off the motor and waited to see what the dog would do. Flyer Frank leaned down and pulled the dog inside.

"I'll bet he wants to rest, too," said Norman.

But Lucky did not seem to be tired. Instead of lying down, he kept pawing Flyer Frank and whining.

"I guess he wants me to go back into the water," the young man remarked. "But I can't go for a little while yet."

Mr. Sampson suggested they put the dog back in the water and maybe he would continue his journey alone. But Lucky would not leave the side of the boat. He paddled in the water just enough to keep afloat.

Honey Bunch sighed. "I guess Lucky won't go unless somebody swims with him," she said.

Steve stood up. "I'll go," he said.

Honey Bunch was delighted. She forgave the big boy at once for all the mean things he had done at Sunrise Beach and on the Island.

Under his clothes Steve wore a pair of bathing trunks. There were so many times during the day when he wanted to go into the water that he always was prepared for a swim.

In a moment he dived overboard. At once Lucky set off on his journey.

In a little while they came to a bell buoy. Lucky paused for a moment and the group in the boat thought perhaps the buoy might have something to do with his search. But a moment later he went on.

At the end of another half-mile, Steve was ready to give up. He came over the side of the boat.

"Guess—you'll—have to—carry on," he pant-ed, speaking to Flyer Frank.

"Okay," the pilot answered, and dived into the water.

As before, Lucky had paused, refusing to go on without a swimmer by his side. Now, he set off again.

"That dog beats me," Mr. Sampson said, shak-ing his head. "He's certainly a strong swimmer! We've come over a mile already."

"How far is it to that land over there?" Honey Bunch asked him, pointing to one of the islands which she could see in the distance.

"That's Pine Tree Island. You saw it yester-day," the lightkeeper replied. "It's about a mile from here."

Lucky certainly seemed to be headed in that direction. Everyone in the boat began to wonder if the dog could make it.

"If he can't," said Mr. Sampson, "we'll take him aboard."

"Then we'll never find out if that's where he was going," Honey Bunch remarked.

"We'll go there and look around anyhow," the lightkeeper assured her.

In another few minutes, Flyer Frank came out of the water and Steve Sampson went in again.

They were sure now that Lucky was headed for the island on which no one was living at the present time.

As they neared the island the dog, though he was now very tired, put on an extra spurt of speed. When they reached the shore, however, and Mr. Sampson beached the motorboat, Lucky collapsed on the sand.

Honey Bunch became fearful as she looked at him. He lay motionless, his eyes staring, his mouth hanging open.

"I guess he's all in," said Flyer Frank. "I'm kind of tired myself, and he swam twice as far as I did."

"Is . . . is Lucky going to be all right?" Honey Bunch asked, a sob in her voice.

At the sound of her voice, Lucky wagged his tail feebly. He tried to get up, but fell back to the sand. The collie kept looking pleadingly at Honey Bunch, and the little girl was sure, for the second time since the dog had come to Shell Horse Island, that he was trying to tell her something.

"Is your master here?" she asked Lucky.

Again the dog wagged his tail ever so slightly.

"Please, Mr. Sampson," said the little girl, "can't we start hunting for Dr. Hopewell?"

"We can," the lightkeeper replied, "but I don't know where to start. This is a pretty sizable place and part of it is covered with brush."

"But you said somebody lives here in the summertime," Honey Bunch reminded him, "so there must be a house."

"I don't see how that will help us," said Mr. Sampson.

Honey Bunch said that if Dr. Hopewell were on the island, he probably would be in the house.

"We can go there and look," he offered.

Mr. Sampson knew where the house was. He led the way through a patch of woods, along an overgrown path. After a while they came to a small, white house and boathouse on the other side of the island. Both were tightly locked.

"Well, I guess your friend is not here, Honey Bunch," said Mr. Sampson.

He was beginning to doubt that the doctor was on the island. He could not figure out, if the man were there, how the Coast Guard could have missed him.

"But Lucky brought us here," Honey Bunch insisted.

The lightkeeper suggested that they call Dr. Hopewell's name. The two men and the children started shouting. There was no answer.

Found!

It was decided that the party would separate into teams to search the island. Flyer Frank would take Honey Bunch and Norman, and Steve and Priscilla would go with their father.

The lightkeeper reached into his pocket and brought out a whistle. He handed it to Flyer Frank.

"If you find Dr. Hopewell," he said, "blow this. I have another whistle. I'll do the same if we find him."

Flyer Frank took Honey Bunch and Norman back through the woods to the beach.

To their surprise, Lucky was not there. Honey Bunch cried out in dismay.

"Oh, Flyer Frank! Where has he gone?"

Flyer Frank pointed to tracks in the sand. "Lucky made these," he said. "We'll follow them and find out where they lead."

He and the children hurried along. Soon the dog's footprints disappeared in the woods.

"Now what are we going to do?" asked Norman.

Honey Bunch began to call loudly. "Lucky! Lucky!"

They all waited for the dog to reply with a bark, but no sound came.

"I'll try calling him," said Flyer Frank.

The pilot had a very strong voice. He shouted so loudly the sound could have been heard anywhere on the island, Honey Bunch was sure. This time, from far off, they could hear the collie's trumpeting bark!

"This way!" said Flyer Frank excitedly.

It was easy for Flyer Frank to make his way through the woods, but Honey Bunch and Norman had a hard time. Both were barelegged, and the bushes and twigs scratched them. But the children did not complain. They were too eager to find Lucky and maybe Dr. Hopewell.

Soon Lucky's barks grew louder. Flyer Frank said he could not be far away.

"Maybe you children had better let me go on alone," he said suddenly.

"Why?" Norman asked.

Flyer Frank did not explain. He was afraid

156

they might come upon Dr. Hopewell badly injured, and he did not want the children to see him in this condition.

"I'll tell you why later, Norman," the pilot answered. "Now, you children stay right here. I'll let you know what Lucky is doing."

The young man hurried on alone. Norman tried to follow, but Honey Bunch held him back. She had guessed why Flyer Frank had gone on alone and tried to explain to Norman.

"I hope the doctor's all right," she concluded.

"If he's not, we can take him to a hospital," said Norman practically.

Suddenly the children could hear Flyer Frank talking. They could not make out the words, but they guessed that he was talking to someone else besides Lucky. As for the dog, he was barking and whining loudly.

"Norman," said Honey Bunch suddenly, "that's a happy bark."

"What do you mean?" the little boy asked.

"Don't you know when a dog's sad and when he's happy? Lucky is happy, I know," Honey Bunch cried in delight.

"Then let's go," said Norman. "We don't have to wait any longer."

Norman did not have a chance to be disobedient, for at that moment Flyer Frank called to the children to come along. The two of them raced to the spot.

"Take it easy," Flyer Frank cautioned, coming up to them. "Dr. Hopewell is here, but he has a broken leg and can't walk."

Honey Bunch and Norman followed the pilot to a little clump of trees whose overhanging branches made a natural shelter. Within it lay Lucky's master.

"Oh, Dr. Hopewell," said the little girl, "I'm so glad you're here! No, I don't mean that. I mean I'm sorry you got hurt, but I'm glad to see you."

The doctor smiled at her. In a rather weak voice he said:

"I'm glad to see you again, Honey Bunch. I'm more glad than you'll ever know. I began to think no one was ever going to find me—and you are the one who found me."

"Oh, we all found you," said Honey Bunch.

Flyer Frank spoke up. "I have been telling Dr. Hopewell how you guessed what was in Lucky's mind, Honey Bunch," he said. "You are really the one who is responsible for our being here. Now, the question is how we are going to get Dr. Hopewell away from this island."

"That's easy," said Norman, who had also spoken to the doctor. "We'll carry him."

"We should have a stretcher," said Flyer Frank. "I believe we can find something up at the house that will do; a blanket, for instance. Mr. Sampson knows the owner, so I'm sure it will be all right for us to go in."

Norman offered to locate Mr. Sampson and his children, but the pilot said he himself would blow the whistle and go to meet them.

"You might get lost," Flyer Frank declared.

Honey Bunch and Norman were left with Dr. Hopewell. They started to ask him questions about how he had come there, but the injured man said he would rather not talk about it just then.

"If I only had the right things to work with," he said, "I could fix up this leg myself."

Lucky would not leave his master's side except to go over and lick Honey Bunch and put up his paw.

"He's trying to thank you," the doctor said, smiling.

"He's a rescue dog again," said Honey Bunch. "He was the one that really rescued you." Then a thought came to her. "Maybe, Dr. Hopewell," she said, "if you have to be in the hospital for a

159

while, getting well, I can take care of Lucky for you. Would you let him go home with me?"

"Gladly," said the young man, "if Lucky will go with you. He's never left my side, and I suppose he'll want to stay in the hospital with me. They probably won't let him, though, so I'll try to make Lucky understand that he's to go with you. Then when I'm well again, I'll come to Barham and pick him up."

Norman thought this would be a fine plan, and he decided then and there that he was going to have Lucky at his house at least part of the time. After all, he had known the dog just as long as Honey Bunch and had shared all the little girl's adventures on Shell Horse Island.

Before he had a chance to mention his idea to Honey Bunch, they saw Flyer Frank coming through the woods with Mr. Sampson and his children. They were carrying two poles, a blanket and several other articles which Honey Bunch could not figure out.

She did not know it, but in order to fly for the Government, Flyer Frank had had to learn first aid. Now he said he would fix up Dr. Hopewell's leg, so that it would not hurt him while he was being carried to the boat and across to Shell Horse Island. He suggested that the children take Lucky to the near-by beach and play until Dr. Hopewell was ready for the trip.

They hunted for sea shells until Flyer Frank called, "We're ready to go now."

Then he and Mr. Sampson led the way, carrying a blanket fastened across the two poles, with Dr. Hopewell lying on it. The children followed.

When they were all in the boat Dr. Hopewell spoke for the first time. "I feel so bad," he said, "that the medicine for the little girl was lost in the ocean."

"Was it a little package that mustn't get damp?" Honey Bunch asked excitedly.

Dr. Hopewell looked puzzled, but said yes.

Honey Bunch and Norman looked at each other. Then both children shouted at once:

"We found the medicine!"

CHAPTER XIV

A DOUBLE GIFT

THE injured doctor looked in amazement at Honey Bunch and Norman.

"What makes you think you found my package of rare medicine?" Dr. Hopewell asked.

Honey Bunch and Norman were becoming more excited by the minute. The little girl asked the man to describe the missing package. When she learned it was about four inches square, and was wrapped in black oilskin, Honey Bunch was sure it was the one Norman had found in the cave.

"Did it say inside, 'DO NOT S'POSE TO DAMPNESS'?" she asked excitedly.

"That's right," the doctor answered, beginning to get excited himself.

Honey Bunch and Norman told him how the package had been discovered near the broken wing of the wrecked plane.

"That's wonderful," Dr. Hopewell said. "I never expected to see that medicine again."

The doctor said he felt better now, and would tell the whole story of what had happened to him since he had left Barham.

"I was delayed getting off," he said, "so I decided to take the shore route. Suddenly I got into a bad wind and could not control my plane.

"I tried going higher, then lower. Then the rain began to come down at a terrific rate. I had flown right into the middle of the storm.

"Suddenly the engines coughed and then stopped. I have no idea where I was when the plane crashed.

"There were only two things I thought about; Lucky and the medicine."

Doctor Hopewell stopped speaking for a few seconds. He reached out to pat Lucky and smile at him. Then he went on with his story.

"My plane hit the water pretty hard. And, believe it or not, the next thing I knew I was on the shore of that little island where you found me."

"Then Lucky saved you!" cried Honey Bunch and Norman together.

The doctor said the dog must have, because there was no one else around. How far Lucky had dragged his master through the water, no one ever would know except Lucky.

"How do you s'pose Lucky got you out of the plane?" Honey Bunch asked the doctor. She remembered how Flyer Frank had slammed the door tight when she and Norman had come to Shell Horse Island.

"We hit the water so hard the door must have been wrenched open," Dr. Hopewell replied. "I was knocked unconscious, but evidently Lucky wasn't."

Again the man stopped speaking for several seconds. Norman could not wait another instant to hear more of the story.

"Then what happened?" the little boy asked excitedly.

Dr. Hopewell said he had lost all track of time and did not know how long he had lain unconscious on the shore. But he had realized that he must get to some shelter before high tide came in.

With Lucky's help he had dragged himself into the woods, hoping to find a house. But his strength had given out and he had collapsed under the clump of trees. When he awakened, Lucky was beside him, but shortly afterward the dog had disappeared.

"That's when he swam to our Island, I guess," said Honey Bunch.

Suddenly an idea came to the little girl. It had been almost two days since the big storm.

"Dr. Hopewell," she said, "haven't you had anything to eat or drink since your air ship-wreck?"

The man smiled and shook his head. He said that he hadn't been hungry, though he had been terribly thirsty.

"Lucky saved my life," he said, petting the great dog curled up close by, "and he would have brought me water too, only he just didn't know how."

"They have swell food at the lighthouse," Norman spoke up. "You can have a good meal as soon as we get there."

Honey Bunch smiled. She remembered the little boy's first meal with the Sampsons. He had not liked it. But since then he had eaten very well, and always asked for second helpings.

During the rest of the trip, the children took turns bringing the doctor up to date on all that had happened to them since leaving Barham.

"I'd say you've had a good many adventures of your own," he remarked, smiling, at the end of the story.

When they docked, all the other people who lived on Shell Horse Island were waiting there to greet them. As Dr. Hopewell was carried up to the Sampson home, Norman hung behind to tell them about finding the man.

During their absence, the new part had come for Flyer Frank's plane, and one of the men had completed the work on the engine of the flying boat. Flyer Frank was delighted, and said the plane would be ready for flight shortly, to take Dr. Hopewell, Honey Bunch and Norman back to Sunrise Beach.

"I believe I'll be able to take off in half an hour," he said. "Honey Bunch, you and Norman had better go around and say good-by to everybody."

Now that it was time for Honey Bunch and Norman to leave, they felt a little sad.

"Maybe I'll never see Priscilla again," Honey

Bunch thought. She liked Priscilla very much and wished she could play with her often.

Priscilla, too, was sorry that Honey Bunch had to leave. There were no other girls on the Island, and she was tired of playing with the boys, who were older than she. The only chance she had to play with other little girls was during the few minutes after school while the Island children waited for the bus to take them to the airport.

"Please come here again," said Priscilla.

"Flyer Frank brought me to visit you," Honey Bunch told her new little friend. "Maybe sometime he'll bring you to visit me. Then you can see Mother again, and Daddy and Mrs. Miller, and my cat and my dog Mr. Reilly."

"Oh, I'd love to," said Priscilla.

She went from place to place with Norman and Honey Bunch so they could say good-bye to the Island people.

When the children had said good-bye to everyone but the Sampsons, they went back to the lighthouse. Mrs. Sampson had a very special dinner ready. She insisted that all those who were going to leave the Island should eat at once.

Dr. Hopewell lay on a couch in the dining room, his dinner on a tray. While he and the children were eating, the doctor told them that the oilskin-wrapped package they had found was indeed the missing medicine. Mrs. Sampson had brought it to him and he had recognized it at once.

"How are you going to get the medicine to the little sick girl up North, now that your leg is busted?" asked practical Norman.

The doctor sighed. "That is the problem right now, Norman," he said. "As soon as we got here, Mr. Sampson radioed a friend of mine, a doctor in one of the hospitals on the mainland, and he has agreed to be ready to take off with the medicine at a moment's notice. The trouble is, we haven't been able to locate a pilot who is free to fly him up North."

"There must be some way to help that little girl," Mrs. Sampson said. "Aren't there any doctors living near her?"

"Not for hundreds of miles," Dr. Hopewell replied. "And anyway, not many doctors know how to use this medicine."

Honey Bunch looked at Flyer Frank and suddenly she had an idea.

"Please," she said to him, "couldn't *you* fly the doctor's friend and the medicine up North to the sick little girl?"

The young pilot thought a moment. "Not in the flying boat; that belongs to the Government," he said. "But I could use my own plane—if only there were someone to fly the Island children back and forth to school while I'm gone."

"There must be some way to work this out," Dr. Hopewell said desperately.

Honey Bunch "put on her thinking cap." She wanted very much to help Lucky's nice master, and somehow she had grown very fond of the unknown little girl who was so sick.

"I know!" Honey Bunch exclaimed suddenly, her blue eyes shining with excitement. "Why can't the Island children play school at home while Flyer Frank is gone? They can do their lessons each day, right on their little lighthouse islands."

Flyer Frank looked doubtful. "Maybe the principal won't permit that," he said.

"I think he would," Honey Bunch said, "to save a little girl's life."

The young flyer agreed that it was a good idea, and hurried to radio the mainland.

Honey Bunch and Priscilla waited anxiously, but later, when Flyer Frank returned, after receiving the answer to his message, the little girls could tell by the broad smile on his face that everything was going to work out all right.

"The principal has given his consent," he announced. "I will fly the doctor and the medicine up North and come right back. Someone else will fly the doctor home, so I'll be gone only this week.

"In the meantime," the young man continued, "the Island children will play school in their own homes. The principal is going to let them know over the radio what lessons they are to study each day."

"What fun!" Priscilla burst out. "I'll bet all the Island children will like that—Steve, most of all!" she added, giggling.

After Flyer Frank had explained that supplies would be carried to the Islands by boat during his absence, Honey Bunch hugged him.

"Oh, Flyer Frank!" she cried. "You're going to be a lifesaving man again!"

Dr. Hopewell was delighted with the arrangement and thanked Honey Bunch for having thought of a way to get the rare medicine to the little girl up North.

Honey Bunch felt very happy about the way everything was turning out. Dr. Hopewell and Lucky and the rare medicine had been found. Then suddenly she thought of something which had not been saved. The doll she had sent to the little sick girl!

"Oh, Priscilla," said Honey Bunch, "would you give away one of your dolls?"

"For you to take home?" asked Priscilla. "I'd love to."

Honey Bunch laughed. "No, not for me," she said.

Then she told Priscilla that somewhere on the bottom of the ocean lay the doll she had planned to give to the little sick girl up North.

"Oh, how dreadful!" exclaimed Priscilla. "That's why you asked me for one of my dolls! To send to her?"

Honey Bunch nodded. The two little girls ran to Priscilla's bedroom and looked over her collection.

"How do you think she'd like this one?" Priscilla asked her. "It's cold up North and this doll—I call her Betty—has on a warm dress and a warm coat and hat."

"I guess she would," said Honey Bunch. She did not know anything about the sick child. Then noticing a lovely boy doll, she said:

"Maybe she'd like him. If she has no brother, this doll could be a brother playmate for her. Let's ask Dr. Hopewell what he thinks."

He told them the little girl had no brothers or sisters.

"Then I'll send my twin dolls," Priscilla announced. "They have red suits."

"They're darling," said Honey Bunch. "Would you really give them away?"

Priscilla smiled. She ran off and brought back the two dolls. Handing them to Flyer Frank, she said, "Please give them to the little sick girl. One is from Honey Bunch, and one is from me."

"I know the little girl will love them," said Dr. Hopewell. "The doll Honey Bunch gave me when I took off is at the bottom of the ocean."

"Oh, I'm so sorry!" said Priscilla.

In a short time, Flyer Frank announced that he was ready to leave. Dr. Hopewell was carried carefully into the flying boat. Then Honey

172

Bunch and Norman said good-bye all over again and climbed in.

Across the water they sped and into the air. Honey Bunch and Norman pressed their faces against the windows and watched Shell Horse Island disappear from view. First the people on it went out of sight. Next, the buildings. And last of all, the lighthouse itself.

As Honey Bunch sat back in her seat, she realized again that even though she had had a wonderful time for the past few days, she would be very glad to see Mother and Daddy again. She wondered if both of them would be at the airport.

When the flying boat descended over Sunrise Beach, and Flyer Frank let down the landing wheels, the little girl could hardly wait to get off the plane.

As they taxied across the field, the children could hear a loud clanging sound. Both of them looked at Flyer Frank and asked what had happened.

"Oh, I guess that's the ambulance for Dr. Hopewell," the pilot answered. "You know he's going to the hospital for a while."

In all the excitement Honey Bunch had forgotten about the hospital. Suddenly she remembered about Lucky, and the possibility the dog would not be allowed to stay in the hospital with his master.

In that case, Lucky was going home to Barham with her for a while!

A moment later the plane came to a stop and Flyer Frank unlocked the door.

"Honey Bunch!" cried a voice.

There stood Mrs. Morton. Honey Bunch ran down the gangplank that had been rolled up to the plane, and hugged her mother tightly.

"Say, how about me?" asked a man's voice.

"Daddy!" screamed Honey Bunch, and jumped into her father's arms.

Norman came in for his share of the gay welcome too. The little boy was sorry his own parents were not there to meet him. But it would not be long before he would be back home in Barham with them, and his face brightened at the thought.

The children watched as Dr. Hopewell was carried on a stretcher from the plane to the ambulance. Lucky never left his master's side for a moment. The ambulance doctor evidently intended that Lucky should ride in front with the driver, but Lucky had other ideas. Before the doctor could step up inside and close the rear door, Lucky made a flying leap and landed inside the ambulance, close to where his master lay. In a moment the driver started the motor and off they went.

"He made it!" cried Norman.

"Lucky's a great dog," said Mr. Morton. And now I think we'd better say good-by to Flyer Frank and start for Barham at once."

"Oh, Daddy!" Honey Bunch cried out. "We can't go yet."

Honey Bunch explained that if the dog could not stay at the hospital, Dr. Hopewell had said she might keep him until the injured man was well again.

"Well," Daddy Morton said, laughing, "that puts a different light on everything! We'll drive to the hospital at once and find out about it."

CHAPTER XV

THE Morton car arrived at the hospital only a few minutes after the ambulance carrying Dr. Hopewell and Lucky.

"I'll go in," said Daddy Morton, "and find out whether or not we're to have the famous dog."

Honey Bunch thought her father never would come out of the big, white building. She and Norman walked up and down, and each time the large door opened, they would rush forward. It was ten minutes before the little girl's daddy appeared.

"He's got Lucky!" Honey Bunch exclaimed, running to meet him.

In the car Honey Bunch threw her arms around Lucky in delight. But Lucky did not move. He just sat quietly beside Honey Bunch, his pointed nose tucked between his two front paws, and his sorrowful brown eyes watching his little friend.

176

"I'm afraid Lucky isn't very happy about leaving his master," Daddy Morton said. He explained that Dr. Hopewell had found it necessary to be very stern with the dog. He had talked with him, saying he must go with Mr. Morton, because dogs were not allowed to stay at the hospital.

Honey Bunch felt very sorry for Lucky. She wanted him to be happy, too.

"Is there any way to make a dog smile?" she asked her mother.

"I've never heard of such a thing," Mrs. Morton replied. "When a dog is happy, he wags his tail."

Honey Bunch watched for Lucky to wag his tail. She talked to him about everything which she thought dogs liked. But still he did not wag his tail.

"Daddy," she said finally, "let's go to the beach before we go home."

"What's in that little mind of yours?" he asked with a smile.

"I'd like to take Lucky down by the waves and talk to him," she said. "Maybe I can make him smile."

Daddy Morton turned the car toward the sandy beach. He parked, and Honey Bunch and

Norman got out with the dog. The two children raced toward the water. Lucky followed slowly.

"Lucky," said Honey Bunch, sitting down on the sand close to the lonely collie, "you see that water out there? Well, you don't have to go in that water any more. You were a lifesaving dog for your master, but now somebody else is going to take care of him for a while."

Lucky squatted on the sand and nuzzled his head against her shoulder. The little girl was sure he was beginning to understand.

"I'll take very good care of you," she said, "all the time you're living with me."

"I will too," Norman promised.

"And your master will come back to you," Honey Bunch added reassuringly.

Suddenly Lucky looked straight into Honey Bunch's eyes. Then he wagged his tail. The next moment the little girl cried out:

"He's smiling!"

Indeed, it did look as if the dog were smiling at her. But before Honey Bunch had a chance to be really sure of this, Lucky began to paw very hard in the sand.

"Gee! He must feel better. He's after something," said Norman.

"Oh, look!" Honey Bunch exclaimed a mo-

178

ment later, as Lucky pulled something white up out of the sand with his teeth and dropped it in front of the little girl. "It's a Shell Horse!"

"We can keep it!" shouted Norman. "Nobody can take this one away from us."

"We can take turns having the Shell Horse," Honey Bunch said, "and we can both take care of Lucky."

But there was still one surprise in store for the little girl which was going to make her always remember her first trip to a lighthouse. Mr. Morton already knew about it.

As he drove into Barham the following day, they noticed flags flying from many of the buildings. There were lots of people on the main street, and a band was playing.

"Oh, Daddy," said Honey Bunch, "is there going to be a parade?"

179

Mr. Morton pulled his car to the curb and stopped. Men and women began to gather around it.

"Here's the famous little girl," said a policeman, as he opened the car door. "Will you please step out, Miss Honey Bunch Morton?"

Before the little girl knew what was happening, the big policeman hoisted her to his shoulder, and all the people around began to clap.

"Now, Honey Bunch," he said, "suppose you tell the people of Barham how you saved the famous Dr. Hopewell."

Honey Bunch was so surprised that for a moment she could say nothing. Then she leaned over and called to Lucky and Norman to come out of the car.

"Can you hold Lucky on your other shoulder?" she asked the policeman. "He's the one that really saved his master. And Norman saved the special medicine."

Everyone clapped.

Lucky seemed to understand what was going on. Of course he was too big to sit on the policeman's shoulder, but he wagged his plumy tail and barked loudly, so that everyone heard him.

After Honey Bunch had told a little bit about the rescue, and a photographer from the newspaper had taken her picture with Lucky and Norman, the Morton family went home.

Mrs. Miller was on the front steps to welcome them. Honey Bunch hugged her and said:

"Oh, Mrs. Miller! I brought you a new word. I had a lallapaloosa of a time."

Mrs. Miller laughed. She knew Honey Bunch meant she'd had a big adventure.

The two playmates were to have another exciting adventure in: HONEY BUNCH AND NORMAN TOUR TOY TOWN.

All of their little friends came over the next day to hear about the lighthouse island and to play with Lucky. The dog was happy now. He knew his master would come back to him. In the meantime, he enjoyed frisking about with Mr. Reilly.

Mrs. Miller served ice cream and homemade cookies. Norman, without asking, went to the

freezer of ice cream and helped himself to a big second portion. At just this moment Mrs. Miller came from the house with another batch of cookies.

"Norman Clark," she said, "your trip didn't change you one bit. You're still a problem child."

Honey Bunch, who was standing near by, heard her.

"Oh, Norman!" she exclaimed. "That's what I meant all the time when I said you were a two-and-two child. I meant you were a problem child."

Norman looked at her. "How do you figure that?" he asked. Then he grinned. "I see," he said, holding up two fingers on each hand. "Two and two make four. That's a problem. Only it's a 'rithmetic problem."

Just as he finished speaking, Lucky gave two short barks, then two more. Honey Bunch laughed.

"You're not a problem dog, Lucky," she said. "You're the most wonderful dog in all the whole, wide world!"